"I've Lived In Hell Since You Left Me, Gini,"

he whispered hoarsely as his tongue ravished her mouth. She was as sweet as honey. "I never stopped loving you. No one, nothing, has ever filled the emptiness in my heart."

His mouth had moved lower and was nuzzling the side of her neck, his lips circling erotically.

"Jordan. Oh, Jordan . . . I'm supposed to be telling you to go. And just look at me." Her low tone quivered with fervent longing.

Her body arched into his, and he felt the completeness of her breathless response. She was soft and pliant in his arms. She drove him wild. He stroked her softly with his roughened hand. It was as if he'd never had a woman in all the years they'd been apart.

"If you really love me, you'll walk out of here tonight and forget me," she murmured helplessly, gasping back a sob.

Dear Reader,

Welcome to Silhouette! Our goal is to give you hours of unbeatable reading pleasure, and we hope you'll enjoy each month's six new Silhouette Desires. These sensual, provocative love stories are both believable and compelling—sometimes they're poignant, sometimes humorous, but always enjoyable.

Indulge yourself. Experience all the passion and excitement of falling in love along with our heroine as she meets the irresistible man of her dreams and together they overcome all obstacles in the path to a happy ending.

If this is your first Desire, I hope it'll be the first of many. If you're already a Silhouette Desire reader, thanks for your support! Look for some of your favorite authors in the coming months: Stephanie James, Diana Palmer, Dixie Browning, Ann Major and Doreen Owens Malek, to name just a few.

Happy reading!

Isabel Swift
Senior Editor

SDRL-7/85

ANN MAJOR
In Every Stranger's Face

Published by Silhouette Books New York

America's Publisher of Contemporary Romance

SILHOUETTE BOOKS
300 East 42nd St., New York, N.Y. 10017

Copyright © 1986 by Ann Major

ISBN: 0-373-05301-0

First Silhouette Books printing September 1986

America's Publisher of Contemporary Romance

Printed in the U.S.A.

Books by Ann Major

Silhouette Romance

Wild Lady #90
A Touch of Fire #150

Silhouette Special Edition

Brand of Diamonds #83
Dazzle #229

Silhouette Desire

Dream Come True #16
Meant To Be #35
Love Me Again #99
The Wrong Man #151
Golden Man #198
Beyond Love #229
In Every Stranger's Face #301

Silhouette Intimate Moments

Seize the Moment #54

ANN MAJOR

is not only a successful author, but she also manages
a business and runs a busy household with three small
children. Among her many interests, she lists travel-
ing and playing the piano—her favorite composer,
quite naturally is the romatic Chopin.

In Every Stranger's Face

Gini . . . Gini . . . Gini . . .

In every stranger's face I still search for you.
You'd come back to me if you only knew
How memories of your sweet, dear loving haunt,
How whispers in the night still painfully taunt.

My fortune and my fame I've come to hate.
Lonely days and lonely nights have been my fate.
Every night I stand on stage and sing.
Yes, Gini, 'cause of you I'm a rhinestone king.

But in every stranger's face I still search for you.
You'd come back to me I'm sure if you only knew
How I still long for the warm sweetness of your arms,
How the memory of a night of wild young love holds charm.

Gini . . . Gini . . . Gini . . .

One

_____

The late-afternoon sky was overcast and drizzling, the temperature of the January day only slightly above freezing. The damp, cold gray made the jumble of unzoned haphazard development along the road appear more depressing than usual, but Gini King had driven this particular stretch too many times to even notice the ugly sameness of it all. Apartment complexes, shopping centers, freeway exchanges and the burned-out shell of a country-western bar were a glistening blur.

Locked in her own tension-producing thoughts, Gini clenched the steering wheel of her ancient blue Valiant with cold-numbed fingers. The heater was out, and her steamy breaths were making the windows frost. She leaned forward and swiped at the windshield to clear it.

How she hated fighting the after-school traffic between Clear Lake, where she taught tenth grade English, and Friendswood, the bedroom community outside the metropolitan sprawl of Houston where she and her thirteen-year-old daughter, Melanie, made their home. But the drive home to Friendswood was an old battle, one of many. For ten years Gini had taught school, commuted, fought to raise her child alone and struggled to make her modest salary cover all her expenses.

It wasn't easy being a divorced woman and trying to do it all alone. What irony that they called this the age of women's liberation!

Something under the Valiant's rusting hood began to rattle ominously, jerking Gini's mind back to the acute situation of her finances. She gave a silent prayer. "Oh, dear, please don't let that sound be anything serious." The thought of still more expensive garage bills made her frown. Worse was the fear she might have to finance a new car, and right now, with Melanie needing braces and sprouting out of her clothes every three months, she just didn't know where she would get the money to make car payments.

The windshield kept fogging, and she kept having to clear a little patch of glass so she could see.

Gini's friends were sympathetic about her difficulties. The statistics about ex-husbands who refused to pay their child support were too staggeringly one-sided for anyone to even suspect that her situation wasn't typical. In the teachers' lounge, Lucy Moreno, Gini's best friend, who happened to be married to a very successful physicist at NASA, would get on her soapbox and rail about the plight of single women in modern society. She loved to deride men for the way they could father children and escape their responsibilities. She would demand to know if Gini knew where her scoundrel ex-husband was, and Gini would shake her head silently, hating herself for the lie.

Oh, she knew.

Sometimes Gini would laugh mirthlessly when she was alone. If her friends only realized the truth, they would not be so sympathetic. They would be thunderstruck, perhaps even jealous. And unbidden would come her own treacherous thought: *You're not like those other women. You don't have to do it alone.*

Then her old fears would consume her, and she would declare aloud as if to convince herself, "Oh, but I do. I do."

Unlike those other women, she lived in fear of her ex-husband's finding her and helping her. The mere thought could fill her with that same nameless dread that had driven her to leave him all those years ago, even when she still loved him.

At thirty-two, despite her massive responsibilities, Gini looked far younger than her age. She was not classically beautiful, but with the softly curling brown hair she wore about her shoulders, and her overlarge tawny doe eyes, she was not unattractive. Her petite body was curved in all the right places. There was a perpetual sweetness in her expression, an utter femininity and grace about her, that gave her a unique charm many far more beautiful women lacked. Her prettiness was of the heart and soul as well as being an external thing, and it was a deeply compelling beauty without any hard edges. People were drawn to her because she was thoughtful and kind, and she had a multitude of friends, both men and women. In her own gentle way she was charismatic.

Gini, however, thought of herself as quite ordinary. She saw herself as a dull, humorless, robotlike worker. The fact that she was so inordinately popular with the teenagers she taught and with everyone who knew her never struck her as anything out of the ordinary. "People are just lonely these days," she would have said, that being one emotion she could sympathize with completely.

Gini swerved onto her own tree-lined street and then turned her car onto the long shell drive. One of her empty trash cans had rolled into the street. She sighed in exasperation. Why didn't Melly ever see—

The sight of overlong grass, a wet newspaper, the unswept porch and the littered carport met her eyes, and as always she fought to ignore these things. Melanie's bike lay in a forgotten heap in the rain.

The level of Gini's tension increased as she got out of the car and picked up the ruined newspaper. She wrapped her coat more tightly around her body as she began to shiver. There was supper to fix, Melanie to see to and papers to grade, and tonight she felt too exhausted to do anything other than collapse. As always, she felt that she had to hurry if she was to get even a fraction of it done.

As she unlocked the back door, she was bombarded by the sound of rock music, and she knew that Melanie had disobeyed her again and was listening to rock videos instead of doing her homework. Blast it! Why couldn't that child—

The thought was never completed. A new video had come on, and the low, husky male drawl hit Gini in the gut like a body blow, draining her of every emotion except her own violent response to that one voice she still loved despite her fervent determination not to. She sank against the door-frame, her very soul in jeopardy. Oh, why couldn't she just forget him? Why did it still hurt so much?

The words of the song came to her as she stumbled in a daze toward the living room. For once, she was too upset to notice that Melanie's homework papers and clothes were scattered across the carpet and furniture. A dirty sock dangled from the windowsill as if it had been enthusiastically tossed there. Samantha, their cat, was in the house, as usual, where she didn't belong.

Gini was completely absorbed by the music. It must be one of his new songs, because she had never heard it before, and somehow she always heard his songs despite the fact that she tried not to. "Gini...Gini...Gini..." Jordan Jacks sang in throbbing lament.

In every stranger's face I still search for you.
You'd come back to me I'm sure if you only knew,
My fortune and my fame I've come to hate...

While listening, Gini had inched her way trancelike into the living room, where she stood watching the tall, compelling, black-haired god on the television screen. Gripping the microphone, his tanned, muscled body clad in blue jeans and a cotton shirt, he catapulted about the stage in a series of acrobatic maneuvers as he sang, exuding a primitive message that lured Gini irresistibly. The erotic passion in his voice and dynamic charisma in his dark handsomeness froze Gini as she devoured his virile features. A hot, electric shiver traced through her body. The whole stage seemed to pulsate with light and sound, and he was at the center of it all.

She could no more have stopped looking at him than she could have stopped breathing. His face was leaner and more rugged than she remembered, but though his hard features had lost all softness of youth, he had retained that wholesome, enchantingly shy manner she remembered from all those years ago. It was a strong face, a face of depth and character, as well as a face of awesome masculinity. She was still drawn to him as powerfully as ever.

The sound of her own name on Jordan's lips, sung with such a shudder of suppressed desire and longing, made her tremble.

So, he hadn't forgotten her completely. She squeezed her eyes shut against the tears that threatened to fall.

Oh, she wished he had! She wished she could forget him, as well, so she could go on with her conventional life. But how did an ordinary woman like herself forget such an extraordinary man? Since their divorce thirteen years ago, every man she'd ever dated she'd compared to him, and never had there been one to lay claim to her heart again. For her, no man could ever be his match.

They'd met in Austin at the University of Texas when they were both students. It had been a time of dissension and change; a time when old values were colliding with new. Flower children in dirty jeans, shaggy hair and beads had set up a perpetual open-air market on the sidewalk on the Drag next to the Co-Op, across the street from the campus. Eastern music whined, and the smell of incense was ever-present. Long-haired girls were wearing mini-skirts. The pill had changed the accepted standards of morality on the campus. It was the dawn of a new and promiscuous age, or so the newspapers said. But Gini had been an old-fashioned girl who didn't care for psychedelic music or the philosophy of free love that was then in vogue. She wasn't on the pill.

Gini met Jordan on a perfectly ordinary blind date their roommates had arranged because neither of them ever dated—a blind date that had proved extraordinary the moment she'd set eyes on him in the Kinsolving Dormitory parlor. When she walked in, her brown hair brushed and shining, wearing her new black plaid gaucho outfit and boots, Jordan was standing in the midst of a crowd of fraternity men in madras shirts and khaki slacks, all waiting for their dates near the telephones. Yet it was as if he were the only man in the room.

Swashbuckling and intense, with his dark, rugged good looks, he was the most compelling man she had ever seen. He was so handsome she imagined him a prince who'd stepped from the pages of a fairy tale. Her eyes met his, and she felt curiously drawn to him as he walked toward her in long, easy strides.

"You must be Gini," he said in a low, drowsy voice that made her bones turn to liquid. He exuded power and yet gentleness at the same time.

"Yes."

She looked into his eyes, and when he smiled a slow, sweet smile that transformed his carved features into an expression of unbelievable tenderness, she knew that the course of her life had suddenly changed.

"You're beautiful," he said, and she was glad suddenly that she had taken such pains with her appearance.

"So are you," she blurted, and then felt gauche because she had no ready phrases to express what she meant. She felt uncertain, tongue-tied. She could have gladly died on the spot.

He gave an astonished laugh. "No one's ever told me that before. That's usually the man's line, you know."

She swallowed. "I imagine that it is, but then I don't know much about lines."

"Do you tell all your blind dates that they're beautiful?" he asked with a return of his devastating smile.

"I—I don't really know."

"Have there been so many that you can't remember?" he teased gently.

At that question she blushed in confusion.

Oh, the misery she felt, and the ecstasy as well. Oh, the painful, exquisite delight of him that made here heart fill with hope and all those little fears.

Later when she looked back upon that night, she came to believe it a mercy that one can feel the terrible vulnerability of first love but once.

His hand circled her waist possessively, and she felt the warmth of his fingers against her flesh. His casual touch felt as intimate as a lover's. She drew a quick, shallow breath as if she were drowning in a swirl of danger and delicious excitement.

"I'm sorry," she began, and lifted her face to his. "I didn't mean anything when I said you were beautiful. I mean, I don't know what to say to you. You see, I hardly ever date. I can't because I have to study all the time. I'm afraid I'm not very experienced."

"Neither am I."

She wasn't prepared for the sudden softening of his tone. The sound of his voice was like velvet sensually caressing her skin. Her heartbeat began to flutter.

They were outside, in the darkness now, standing on the steps above the curb; the brick dormitory loomed behind them.

In the shadows he seemed different, more awesome somehow. Moonlight was gleaming in his ebony hair, but his handsome face was half-hidden in the gloom, giving him a mysterious air. Though she couldn't see his eyes, she could feel his hot, ravishing gaze move lingeringly over her. She could almost imagine him a buccaneer in a more romantic age.

He would have been magnificent, with a black cloak thrown over his broad shoulders. He towered over her, and she was more aware than ever of what a magnificently virile male animal he was. She scarcely came to his shoulders, and the power of him made her feel so pleasantly tiny and feminine. Yet, at the same time, she was conscious of the tantalizing sensation of fear. Despite what he'd said, she was out of her depth, and he was not.

"I wonder if you were making fun of me, Mr. Jacks," she began haltingly. "I find it difficult to believe that you're as inexperienced as I am."

"Oh, but I am," came the treacherously silken sound of his voice. "I don't usually date...girls like you." He smiled then, a brilliant, flashing smile.

A ripple of excitement went through her. "And what kind of girls... do you usually date?" she queried breathlessly.

He hesitated, but only briefly, as though he wondered how to answer her. "I usually date girls I can go out with, have a good time with and forget," he replied.

Even on that first night there was a blunt honesty in their relationship that they would both come to treasure later.

"And I'm different?" she asked shyly, tremblingly aware of him.

"Very."

"In what way?"

"For one thing, you're a virgin."

His eyes swept her slim body, and she felt a warmth heat her body. "How could you possibly know that?" she cried, embarrassed. Then her temper ignited, and she began in a fiercer tone, "Why, you have no right to talk to me like that."

"You asked the question," he answered blandly. "I assumed you wanted the answer. You're also different, Miss Fisher, in that you are quite unforgettable." The hard line of his mouth softened into that enchanting smile of his that could so dazzle her.

Her anger dissolved instantly in the soothing balm of his compliment, and she rather hated herself for being so easy for him to manipulate.

He pulled two cardboard strips from his pocket and waved them in front of her eyes. "I have tickets to the football game, but suddenly I don't particularly care about being part of that mob scene," he said, "unless, of course, you want to. I know a quiet place on the river where we could dance and talk and..." His gaze drifted to her mouth. "But where would you like to go tonight?"

If just that bold, hot look in his eyes could make her shiver, what would happen when they were alone, dancing and talking? It was intoxicating to imagine him pulling her against his hard chest, their bodies swaying rhythmically together to the soft strains of romantic music.

"Maybe the football game would be nice, safer," she blurted. Oh, why had she said that last word?

"Your mother must have taught you to think like that," he said. "I'm not in the mood to play it safe. Not tonight. Are you?"

"I—I don't know." Then, impulsively, Gini said, "I think if I were wise I would run back inside my dorm and leave you to the kind of girls you're used to. I'm afraid we couldn't possibly have much in common. I'm sure you'll be bored and disappointed."

He threw back his head and laughed. "I have no intention of being bored or disappointed."

"Oh?"

"And I will try very hard to achieve...er...a common bond," he drawled lazily.

"That's exactly what I'm afraid of."

"How proper you're beginning to sound, Gini. I think that must mean you're beginning to feel quite improper."

She flushed a telling crimson. Oh, it was all too obvious he knew far too much about women. "I really do think—" she began.

He didn't let her finish. "Don't you want to go out with me?"

"Oh, yes, but—"

"Then will it be the game or dancing?"

His sparkling eyes studied her face. She thought surely he must see every secret in her soul. She looked away.

"Anywhere. With you," she finally allowed herself to admit. Perhaps she should have been coy or used her feminine wiles. But she couldn't. Even in that first hour there was an extraordinary honesty between them.

"That's exactly the way I feel, Gini, but most girls would never be so honest about their feelings. Hasn't anyone ever schooled you in the advantages of playing hard to get with a man?"

"I've never been very interested in games," she murmured.

"Neither have I." His voice was low and disturbingly sensual.

Suddenly she felt his hands on her shoulders. He drew her into his arms and lowered his dark head to hers and kissed her quickly, softly and then urgently. She felt the warmth of his tongue as it slid against hers to explore her mouth. The moment he touched her, she felt breathlessly on fire, feverishly alive. He released her, and she sighed in aching disappointment.

"I had to do that, Gini." His hot, dark gaze lingered on her lips.

"I know," she whispered.

Still warm from his kiss, her lips were moist and expectantly full and inviting.

He groaned. "Don't look at me like that if you don't want to be kissed again." Then he drew her more tightly to him than before.

She was as eager as he. She felt the hardened length of his body pressing against her, the muscular strength of him, the heat of him, the force of his thighs against her untutored body. She did not mind even that intimacy, for she'd known the instant she saw him that he was special.

"There ought to be a law against this," he murmured. Then he kissed her again, and this time he couldn't let her go.

His lips moved across her upturned face, gently, passionately. She was drowning, soaring, her passion as blazing as stardust, as overwhelming as the sun blotting out all darkness. She was his, and he was hers. Nothing mattered except him—and his fierce desire that had changed them both with one kiss.

She was his woman. Forever, she would only be his. They were twin souls in a universe filled with strangers, two beings consumed by the flame of a single passion.

At last he released her, and she could feel his giant body trembling against hers. "I want you." His voice was strangely harsh, even as his fingers tenderly smoothed her tousled hair from her brow. "More than I've ever wanted any woman."

"And I want you. I've been waiting for you all my life," she admitted freely. It felt as if her life had only just begun since he had come into it.

"I want to know everything about you," he said.

"There's not much to know."

"Only a lifetime," he murmured.

"Where do I begin?"

"With this moment. What are you feeling right now?"

"I'm afraid," she said shakily.

"So am I." He dropped his arm casually about her waist and drew her against him.

"But why would you be afraid?"

He did not answer; he merely kissed her again, more gently than before, but there was commitment and acceptance of that commitment now. There was also the tantalizing promise of surrender because she held nothing back, and they both knew he could have her, whenever he wanted her.

From their first kiss, their love was inevitable.

It was only later that they would learn how little they had in common, how terribly mismatched they were, how different their goals in life were. By then it was too late.

That night they talked for hours in the rustic country-western dance hall that overlooked a glistening Town Lake. They ate barbeque and potato salad, drank Lone Star beer and held hands beneath the folds of a checkered tablecloth, pouring out the secrets of their hearts, rejoicing in every new piece of knowledge they learned about each other.

A Harvard business graduate, Jordan was in his last year of law school and on the law review, while she was a freshman struggling to make B's and C's.

"I've always wanted to be a teacher," she admitted, "more than anything. I know this is going to sound silly, but I love kids. And I want to work with them."

"It doesn't sound silly."

The sincerity in his velvet drawl made her go warm all over. His intense, dark gaze wove a spell she would not long be able to resist. Quickly, she changed the subject from herself to him. Too quickly.

"When did you first realize you wanted to be a lawyer, Jordan?"

His expression froze, and for a long while he made no reply. He toyed with his fork and then tossed it aside.

"Did I say something wrong?" she asked urgently, feeling that somehow she'd unwittingly said the wrong thing.

"No, Gini. It's nothing you said." He spoke in a funny, dead tone, and his hand that gripped hers beneath the table tightened. "My father is a lawyer," he began at last. "He's always wanted me join his firm. It's a very prestigious position." He released her hand.

"That sounds wonderful."

"That's what everybody always says," he said grimly. "Come on, Gini, let's dance."

He swept her against his body, and only then did his tension begin to ease. Beneath moonlight flooding through the windows, and to the raucous sound of fiddles and banjos, they swirled across the battered oak floor. They were the only couple on the dance floor. He held her close against his broad-shouldered frame, and she reveled in the feel of him, the scent of him, the magnificence of him. His hands held her captive against his powerful chest, and slowly the undulating pressure of their entwined bodies swaying together aroused a sharp-set hunger within her. As though he felt it, he held her even more closely and brushed her temple with his lips in a long, smoldering kiss.

It seemed a dream to be in his arms, to belong to him, to be cherished by him. She was afraid that any minute she might awaken and he would be gone, and she would be alone. Before she had met him, she had accepted her life without him. But now, if he were to leave her, it would seem unspeakably dreary. His presence lit her world with a new and brilliant radiance.

They waited a week before they made love. During that time they were together every minute they were not in class.

They ate dinner every night in the Student Union, studied together in the library and parted each night with greater reluctance than the evening before. They told each other their attraction was mental as well as physical. In her, he saw compassion and warmth. She found his mind brilliant. But in reality, the major attraction they found in one another, the most fascinating enticement between them, was purely sensual, and these feelings rapidly built to an unbearable climax.

At dawn, after an all-day date the next Saturday, he took her home to his room. Overwhelmed by his love for her, he was shy and gentle with her as he carried her inside, swept aside the mountain of law books that had cluttered his rumpled bedspread and laid her on his bed.

"Where's your roommate?"

"He went to College Station for the weekend."

A breathless excitement coursed through her. She was unable to speak. Her long-lashed eyes lifted, bright and startled and yet not startled at all, and met Jordan's heated gaze.

The tremulous silence lengthened between them.

Abruptly he caught her shoulders and pulled her toward him. Her body melted into his. She was trembling even before he kissed her. Tentatively, she lifted her arms around his shoulders, drawing him closer, her fingertips curling in the ink-black curls that brushed against his collar.

He began to undress her, deftly unbuttoning her gauzy blouse while he kissed the graceful slimness of her pale throat, unzipping her velvet skirt while he murmured soft endearments that stilled her fears. His devouring gaze ranged the slender length of her radiant, opulent beauty. She was shiveringly aware of everything he did, and she flushed at the intimacies she allowed him.

Gently he swept aside several brown tendrils of hair that lay in gleaming arabesques against her hot cheek. He gathered her warm body in his arms.

She felt a rush of the most powerful emotion she had ever known. It was as though she hovered on the brink of some monumental discovery. There was the intense, tantalizing excitement of the unknown between them—the allure of the mysterious, the wondrous sensation of expectancy.

The fragrant scent of freshly mown grass and the smoke from leaves being burned nearby drifted in through the partially opened windows.

Soon they lay naked in each other's arms amidst tangled sheets and rumpled pillows. His bedspread lay crushed at their feet. Gini's gauzy blouse, velvet skirt and filmy lingerie trailed forgotten, half on and half off the bed.

Jordan's fingertips caressed the faint curve of her belly. "And I thought virgins were an extinct species on campus," he said.

"Don't rub it in," she whispered. "It's not something I want advertised."

His hands explored the velvet creaminess of her skin. "You should be proud of it."

"Proud 'cause no guy ever wanted me?" She looked up at his face and then arched her back so that the tip of her breast met his mouth. She moved enticingly as he suckled first one nipple and then the other until she began to tremble as a wave of new feeling washed over her.

The soft light from his small desk lamp played gently over her golden body. "You don't believe that any more than I do," he said. "Any man would want you."

"But I hadn't met you."

"Oh, Gini." He gazed deeply into her eyes. "Gini." His hands moved lovingly over her silken body, touching her everywhere, until her skin seemed to glow from his touch and he was on fire with need.

"I want you to make love to me all night," she purred, stretching voluptuously as he traced the length of her thigh with his lips.

He reached across her and pulled the chain on the lamp. The room melted into darkness.

"That won't be difficult. The sun will be coming up soon."

Their laughter joined in a melody of joyous sound before his hard body covered hers. Every inch of him was sinew and muscle against her delicately soft femininity. Then there was awed silence as he looked into her eyes and kissed her gently before he possessed her. And then there was only the sound of love, the smothered cries of passion. Despite her innocence she no longer knew shyness with him. She knew only the languorous splendor of yielding fulfillment.

Afterward, he became possessive of her, and she of him. The glorious red-and-gold autumn belonged only to them. They were young lovers lost to the world, lovers who lived and breathed only to be together. Again and again in the days and nights that followed they gave in to their insatiable desire for each other, drawing pleasure from every transient hour spent in each other's presence, from the simplest touch or caress, from the most casual gesture of affection, from everything new they shared together. Every moment spent together was cherished no matter how seemingly insignificant. She surrendered to her needs with the greedy compulsion of a passionate woman who had been starved all her life for such sensuous ecstasy. Now she knew what she had wanted even on that first night when she'd seen him in Kinsolving Dormitory. She had longed for the wildness of his powerful body on hers, for the shameless abandon of belonging to him.

Oh, the terrible, terrible power of young love. It was filled with a thousand little agonies in the midst of ecstasy. He had only to smile at another girl, to arrive five minutes late at her dormitory for their date, to forget to call, and she would be besieged with doubts.

They married in six weeks, giving little thought to anything except the mad, blind passion between them. Too late she'd begun to realize the magic of his musical ability and the disparity between his brilliance and her mediocrity. To support them, he had to take a part-time job at night singing in a bar. He wrote his own songs, and every night he sang, a larger audience showed up to hear him than the night before. When his voice rasped husky eroticisms to a torrid beat, the crowd went wild. On stage, he was magic. His shyness left him. He was a born entertainer.

His parents had taught him that he should become a lawyer like his father and grandfather and great-grandfather, even though his heart and real talent lay in music. Jordan's stolid, conservative parents deplored the wild lives of rock stars and had convinced him that only degenerates went into such a field, and that if one wasn't a degenerate when one began such a career, one soon would be. Gini, whose parents were middle-class ranchers, had raised her with the same conservative views.

Then one warm Saturday night, Felicia Brenner, with her permanent California suntan and golden hair, walked into that nondescript bar on Sixth Street just off Congress Avenue where Jordan worked. A friend had told her about the mesmerizing talent and molten voice of the darkly handsome newcomer who sometimes sang there. Felicia later told Gini that she'd meant to order one drink and leave, but the minute she stepped inside the shabby establishment she felt the crowd's response to Jordan. When her skin began to crawl with excitement at the primitively male, velvet sound, she recognized his extraordinary talent. She stayed until he finished his set, leaving her drink untouched on the scarred mahogany bar. Recently divorced, wealthy in her own right as the daughter of a television station owner and ferociously ambitious, Felicia instantly approached Jordan, thrust her gaudy gold business card into his hand and offered to represent him.

Jordan was backstage, wiping the perspiration from his face with a towel as he leaned against the wall. His black hair hung across his forehead. There were shadows beneath his magnetic dark eyes. He was exhausted from the pressure of classes, long hours of studying and working nights. He read the card in amazement and laughed at Felicia's offer as he slid his arm possessively around Gini as if to assert that only one woman had any claims to him.

"You don't understand," he murmured, too tired to try to be polite. "I'm not really a singer. I'm in law school. I have a wife. There are other commitments that take priority over my music."

Felicia lit a cigarette and regarded them for a long moment. Gini felt defenseless and out of her element beside the two of them. "No, Mr. Jacks, *you* don't understand. You're a singer. A genius. I've never heard music exactly like yours."

Jordan threw back his head and laughed. "You're crazy."

"Don't laugh, Mr. Jacks. If there's one thing I know, it's music. You've got the appeal of Elvis, and your music is as stirring and original as the Beatles. You can be big in the music business, Mr. Jacks. Lawyers are a dime a

dozen." Felicia's predatory gaze fell on Gini. "No commitment should come before your music."

"What you're saying is incredible."

"You're the one who is incredible. I'm only one of the
first to know it. If you let me help you, soon the whole
world will know it and love you."

"Sorry. Not interested. I have all the love I'll ever need."
He'd swept Gini into his dressing room and closed the
door, but instead of kissing her, Jordan had asked, his eyes
brilliant with interest, "Do you think there's a chance she
knows what she's talking about, darling? Or is she as crazy
as I think she is?"

And it was then that Gini realized his heart was in his
music and would never be in a law career. For the first time
she felt afraid.

"Yes," she whispered, "I do think she knows what she's
talking about. You're good. I mean, really good."

"That's not the kind of life I want for us," he'd said
roughly, but there was an edge of regret in his husky voice
as he pulled her into his arms, the musky smell of his
heated body filling her nostrils like the most powerful
aphrodisiac. The minute their bodies touched, she felt his
muscles tense, his heart beat faster. Their kiss lasted for a
very long time.

Felicia didn't take no for an answer. She bombarded
Gini with calls, unerringly sensing Gini was the weakest
point, the place to attack. Felicia's message was always the
same. Jordan was a musical genius, and his career should
be music despite the hazards. Felicia had connections in
the entertainment business. "You're holding him back,
Mrs. Jacks. It's only because of you that he rejects what
he really wants."

Gini realized that there was an element of truth in Felicia's arguments no matter how hard Jordan fought to deny it, and unlike his parents, she began to gently encourage him to fulfill his potential. She didn't reveal that she was secretly becoming terrified of his talent and where it might lead them.

For her, Jordan would have denied his talent, but she was unable to let him make that sacrifice. More than anything she wanted him to be happy. But she was as terrified as his parents of the wild things she'd read about rock stars. And as she met more and more people in the music field, she came to realize that she couldn't stay with him if he chose to be an entertainer. She could not fit into that glamorous but erratic lifestyle. Her presence would only hold him back, and she knew that eventually he would see their love as an impossible and mutually destructive force. To let him fulfill the destiny he'd been born to, she had to divorce him quickly, before their lives were hopelessly mired.

Gini didn't know she was pregnant until after she'd left him, and then she decided that a baby would only bind him to her. It would not be fair to either of them for her to tell him. But her pregnancy had been an agony of loneliness.

After their divorce Jordan Jacks's success had been meteoric, and for thirteen years he'd remained on top. His name had been linked with every beauty in Hollywood, but he'd never married again. He never gave personal interviews, so all she could read about him were journalists' pieced-together stories. There had even been one paternity suit, which he'd fought, and a titillating scandal or two, and these had almost convinced Gini that she could never have fit into the kind of lifestyle Jordan was forced to live. He constantly traveled, while she was the type who liked to stay in one place. Over and over she'd told herself there was no way their marriage could have survived.

But these rationalizations were little comfort to her when she felt achingly alone. Through the years it had been hard raising Melanie without a father. Sometimes she felt the most terrible guilt because she had denied Jordan his child, just as she felt guilty for denying Melanie her father. She'd had to turn her back on every person she'd ever known and make a whole new life for herself and her baby.

The decision she made had been difficult, but it was even more difficult to live with. The woman who suffered the consequences of that choice was no longer the girl who had walked away from Jordan, and there were times when she secretly wondered if she had done the right thing.

Her secret was eating her alive.

Two

Gini...Gini...Gini...

The velvet male sounds died away as Gini came out of her reverie and found herself still standing in her shabby living room. She felt lost and disoriented, gripped by the terrible past she'd spent a lifetime trying to forget.

Jordan finished his song and bowed to his cheering fans. Slowly he straightened his body, lifting his dark face to the lights. Gini's gaze locked with the bold blackness of his eyes, those beautiful, magnetic eyes fringed with the thickest of lush, curling sable lashes, eyes too beautiful to belong to the ruggedly handsome face they belonged to. Surely no woman alive was immune to the sensual message in those eyes, Gini thought weakly, and from the crazed shouts of his adoring fans, no woman was.

He smiled that shy half smile she remembered so well, and her heart felt suddenly as if it would burst. If only... No, she had been right to leave him. He exuded sex appeal. He had star presence. How could such a man who belonged to the millions ever belong to one woman?

"Why, Mother, you're crying," came Melanie's soft voice from the tattered, overstuffed chair. She was amazed because, like many teenagers, she rarely saw her mother as a flesh-and-blood human being.

"No, I'm not," Gini denied, fleeing, even as the mother in her took over, and she managed a series of predictable, rote commands. "Turn off the TV and bring the trash cans in, put your bike in the carport and start your homework, young lady."

"Aw, Mom," Melanie protested as she reluctantly dragged herself from her slouched state of relaxation and turned off the set. "I just got in."

In her own room, Gini collapsed on her unmade bed, oblivious to the clutter she normally would have been efficiently neatening at this hour in the day. Her whole body felt on fire from having seen and heard Jordan's stirring new video. There was a terrible sadness in Jordan's song, and she was filled with a bitter sensation of regret in response to it. Was it possible he wasn't as happy as she'd always believed he'd be without her? Why couldn't he have just been a lawyer or a teacher or anything normal? Why did it have to end the way it had?

Oh, but how sinfully, devastatingly beautiful he still was with that sweet, shy smile of his that made him look so vulnerable. His lips were full and sensual. She could almost feel their touch on sensitive flesh. She remembered how he'd always kissed her with that all-consuming passion that was part of his nature. She remembered how his lips had lingered so caressingly upon every secret, intimate place of her body until she was wild with desire. That same passion that made him a great musician had made him a great lover.

Who did he sleep with now? What woman knew the blistering heat of his mouth, the power of that lean, masculine body as he clasped her to him with his strong arms? Who heard his frenzied groan of passion? What body arched into his as once hers had?

Shaking fingers wadded the edge of her pillowcase. Oh, it was unbearable to think of him with anyone else. She would drive herself crazy if she thought of it.

She got up and began to attack with ferocity the task of preparing dinner, straining to prove at least to herself that she would not be mastered by this willful, hopeless desire for the one man she could never have.

At dinner Melanie said, "You're awfully quiet tonight, Mom."

"Am I? I guess I'm tired. The kids were kind of wild today. Brad especially. While I was busy, he climbed a ladder and hung by one hand a hundred feet over the stage. When I yelled at him to get down, I nearly made him fall. It was terrible. We're acting out *Julius Caesar*, you know, and I'm an English teacher, not a director."

"Why'd you say you weren't crying a while ago when you were?" Melanie asked, staring at her mother intently. "Was it 'cause that song was about a girl named Gini?"

Gini's fork rattled against china, but she managed a calm tone. "It just seemed silly, to cry. That's all. And over a stupid song."

"Jordan Jacks is really something—and at his age."

"For heaven's sake, he's only thirty-eight," Gini snapped.

"That's old for a rock star. There's only a few that can hang in there, like Mick Jagger, Bruce Springsteen and him. Hey, but how'd you know his age?"

"I—I..." Gini looked up, startled, and then quickly masked her fear. "I guess I read it somewhere."

"I didn't know you ever read about rock stars, Mom."

"I don't. It must have been in the paper or something."

Melanie pushed her long black hair out of her face. Her dark eyes from beneath dense lashes, eyes so like those other eyes, studied her mother, and just for a moment Gini shivered. The daughter was too dangerously like her father, but no matter what, Melanie must never, never know the truth.

"Well, you're acting like you have a crush on him, Mom."

"Don't be ridiculous!" Gini sputtered furiously, turning scarlet. "And I wish you'd think about something besides that awful music and those videos. Your room looks like a nightmare with all those ridiculous posters of rock stars papering your walls. And you know you're supposed to come straight home from school and start your homework. Instead you're either playing your guitar or listening to that interminable music, and I don't know why I have to tell you this every day."

"All the other kids do the same thing."

"That's got to be the lousiest excuse in the world."

"It's the truth. Anyway, I don't see anything wrong with liking music."

Gini took a deep breath to steady herself. "It's just that, Melanie honey, I want you to be interested in different things. All your life, it's only been this one thing—rock. It really sells kids the wrong message about life; to be irresponsible."

"Since you never listen to it, how do you know? You ought to be happy I like something. Lots of kids do drugs, you know, and sex."

"Oh, Lord," Gini groaned wearily, resigning from the confrontation. "Sex and drugs. The perpetual nuclear bombs you teenagers use to fight your battles. We parents are not supposed to expect anything out of you. We're supposed to die with gratitude if you aren't absolutely horrible. Is it so wrong of me to hope that you'll amount to something? Girls can be doctors and lawyers."

"Well, I don't want to be a doctor or a lawyer, Mother! And I don't want to be a schoolteacher either! I want to do something with my music." With that, Melanie pushed her chair back from the table.

"I've told you and told you, that's no kind of life for a girl like you!"

"I'm not going to listen to you anymore. You're trying to run my life! And that's something I'll never let you do."

As Gini watched her storm down the hall with that air of melodrama teenagers can instinctually and effortlessly attain, a tide of frustration washed over her. Why had she confronted the music issue so directly? Melanie was as stubborn and strong willed as her father, and if she was told no, that only made her more determined. The last thing Gini wanted to come home to after a hard day at school was a quarrel with her own teenager, but it seemed to be happening more and more frequently these days.

Mother and daughter passed the rest of the evening in silence, with Gini washing the dishes and grading papers, and Melanie laboring over a science project. When Gini went into Melanie's room to tell her good-night, Melanie gripped her mother's hand fiercely in the darkness, her childish anger gone.

"I'm sorry I was so awful at dinner," she whispered. "You were thinking of Daddy, weren't you? That's why you cried."

Gini nodded mutely.

"What was he like? We don't even have one picture. You won't ever even talk about him."

Gini lifted her gaze to the most dazzling wall poster in the room and met the compelling irony in Jordan's sardonic black gaze. In her present mood, his white smile seemed defiant. Clad in dark jeans, his long, muscular legs were thrust widely apart. His frilled shirt was slit halfway to the waist, revealing a bronzed chest matted with dark curled hairs. A towel dangled from his neck. Every inch of him seemed vitally alive and earthily masculine, and Gini felt her blood stir as a queer thrill swept her.

Quickly she looked away. "He was very special, darling," she said quietly, her voice thin and choked. "But we were wrong for each other." She kissed Melanie lightly on the cheek and rose to go. "If we had stayed together we would have destroyed one another."

Melanie stared after her mother in puzzlement and then turned and regarded the poster of Jordan Jacks for a long moment. She was filled with a mysterious sensation of expectancy, as if she stood on the edge of some monumental understanding. There was something about Jordan Jacks that really got to her mother, no matter what her mother willingly admitted. Not that it was anything to be ashamed of. All the girls at school thought Jordan Jacks was quite a hunk. But was her mother's preoccupation like a high-school crush, or did it go much deeper? What was it about Jacks that disturbed her mother so?

Melanie turned on her radio and put her headset on so that her mother wouldn't know she was listening to it.

Jordan's husky voice was singing, "In every stranger's face I still search for you."

As Melanie stared drowsily into those black eyes so like her own, she was deeply moved.

If only she could understand. . . .

She fell asleep, his famous half smile on her lips.

In her own room, Gini lay awake, thinking about Jordan's new video, seeing again in her mind his every gesture, his gentle half smiles, hearing again his music and the disturbing sensuality of his husky voice. At last she drifted into a fitful sleep, and he haunted her even then.

Her dreams were filled with a tall dark man whose bold hot music wrapped her as he sang only to her. In a floating white nightgown, she was running through a blur of lime-green trees beside a sparkling river, trying to escape him, but everywhere she turned, there he was. Then at last she stood still like a frightened fawn, waiting, her large eyes uncertain, her pulse racing, and he was running toward her, his arms outstretched. He swept her high against his chest, lifting her, swirling her, pulling her hard against him, burying his face in the soft fall of her hair.

"Love me again. Please, Gini. Don't ever leave me," his beautiful voice begged against her luxuriant hair as his hands roamed her body.

His desire was like a raging torrent as he shredded her diaphanous nightgown, his hands burning to touch her bare flesh, to cup her satin breasts.

She couldn't fight him any longer, and with a soft cry of pleasure she surrendered to the warm lips devouring her very soul, to the passion she'd spent a lifetime trying to live without.

The long dream-filled night was wild and wanton. Together they enjoyed every imaginable pleasure. He was a delicious thickness inside her, a moving stirring presence that possessed her body with fiery passion, learning her, using her, bringing her exquisite, mindless rapture.

The next morning when she awoke alone, she felt worse than ever before. How could she go on living without him? But she had to. There was Melanie.

She was going to have to make herself start dating again. It was ridiculous to go on mooning for a man she had decided she couldn't have. She thought of Dave Richardson, the handsome basketball coach where she taught, and decided that the next time he asked her out she would accept.

When Gini arose there were dark shadows beneath her eyes. She flinched at the sight of her pale, drawn face in her mirror. This was why she never listened to Jordan's songs, never deliberately looked at his pictures, never wanted to think of him. When she did, he invaded her heart and soul so completely that she was so utterly miserable she could scarcely function.

She dressed quickly and left the house a little before six-thirty, anxious to get to work. Only at school could she completely forget Jordan when she was in one of these moods. She called a swift goodbye to her daughter as she opened her umbrella and darted into the darkness toward her car. Melanie would ride to her school with friends who would drop by later.

Rain was falling in sheets as Gini switched on her headlights and backed down the drive; she had to drive carefully because there was already a lot of traffic, even at this hour.

Gini was tired, and she had to strain to see the road. The windshield began to fog, and she wiped at it. Then she switched on the radio, and Jordan's mesmerizing voice filled the car, electrifying her.

> . . . My fortune and my fame I've come to hate,
> Lonely days and lonely nights have been my fate . . .
> But in every stranger's face I still search for you . . .

Her vision blurred as a wave of powerful emotion burst

inside her. Or perhaps it was only the windshield fogging again. She would never know. At just that moment a car weaved at high speed from the opposite lane and roared toward her head-on. She screamed and swerved. Old tires skidded on rain-slick pavement, and her car plunged out of control off the road. The ditch was deep, and her car rolled over and over like a broken toy thrown carelessly by an angry child, until at last it stopped in the water-soaked field, its headlights beaming upward at a peculiar, slanted angle.

In the upside-down car, Gini lay in an agony of pain, just on the fringes of consciousness, as water and mud oozed inside the mess of twisted steel, torn upholstery and shattered glass. The radio was still playing, and Jordan's voice singing the last refrain cruelly taunted her. "Gini . . . Gini . . . Gini . . ."

Scarcely conscious, she lay in a shadowy, timeless limbo of pain. She couldn't move. She couldn't breathe. The smell of gasoline enveloped her like a thick cottony fog. Dimly, she was aware of hard crashing sounds outside, of glass being kicked in by a heavily booted leg, of a door being wrenched open, of water and mud seeping inside, covering her beautiful, soft brown hair. Hard hands clasped her shoulders, and she screamed in a paroxysm of pain.

"Lord, I hate to move her!"

"Hurry!" There was fear in the second voice.

She was lifted and carried. There seemed to be lights and sirens everywhere. Then an explosion of sound and heat engulfed them as her car burst into flame.

"Jordan," she murmured faintly. "Jordan . . . I want Jordan. Please. . . ."

As if from another universe, she heard a man's gruff voice. "What did she say?"

"I don't know, but she's hurt bad. We've got to get her to a hospital quick, or it'll be too late."

It was four thirty-five in the morning in Malibu, California, when Gini's car skidded off that rain-slick road in Texas, and she screamed for the only man she had ever loved.

Jordan Jacks sprang awake, wrenched by the vivid, irrational terror of his nightmare. He sat up in his massive bed, his muscular body soaked with perspiration despite the chill air. For an instant he thought he was going to be sick, but the awful nausea passed and left him feeling curiously weak. Wearily, he ran a large bronzed hand through the black hair that tumbled over his brow.

Damn! But that dream about Gini had been real! That last scream had torn his heart. She'd seemed so heartbreakingly alive in his dream. So fragile and so dangerously near death.

The dull lifetime ache he'd learned to live with hit him in the stomach, and his vivid terror was replaced with the terrible reality he'd had to accept.

She was dead. She had been for over ten damn years. Funny that he could still ache for her, that sometimes he still dreamed of her. Once, right after he'd gone back to Texas and found out she'd died, Jordan had even gone to a psychiatrist, though that was a secret he carefully guarded. Jordan had explained to the doctor that he just didn't feel as if Gini were dead, and the doctor had said that that was because he'd learned about it after she had been dead for more than a year, and because he hadn't gone to her funeral. His only advice had been to go to the cemetery where she was buried. But hell, even the small consolation of being able to put flowers on her grave had been denied him. When he confided to her parents that he wanted to visit her grave, they'd looked uncomfortably alarmed before her father blurted the terrible truth; they'd had her cremated and poured her ashes over the Gulf of Mexico.

Damn! His Gini cremated. She *should* seem so utterly gone. Why didn't she?

Not liking the morbid path of his thoughts, he glanced at his watch. Hell, it was only four-thirty and he hadn't gotten to sleep until one. He'd wanted to sleep late so he'd be fresh for his recording session that afternoon.

He punched two buttons by his built-in bed, and a bank of curtains screening a vast glass wall slid open as if by magic, revealing a panoramic coastline view. He deactivated the security system and closed-circuit television monitors. Then he got out of bed and strode out onto the balcony of his villa that was a marvel of the most sumptuous luxury even for Malibu.

The two-acre grounds were landscaped with natural rock outcroppings, large trees, orchards, three waterfalls, two koi ponds, a swimming pool, whirlpool and a tennis court. Jordan had long ago grown oblivious to these surroundings, as he was to all the trappings of his immense wealth.

Seven years ago his business manager, Felicia Brenner, had demanded that he purchase a house. With Felicia to oversee the project, he'd let her hire an architect, a team of decorators and landscape architects, and a horde of other experts to redo the house, but the mansion, with its 24-karat-gold fixtures, Italian travertine marble flooring, custom carpeting, and walls upholstered in brown suede and raw silk, had never felt like his. He simply lived in it—when he stopped working long enough to live anywhere.

Felicia, however, adored it, and once he'd said jokingly to her, "Then you should live in it."

"That's what I've been thinking for a very long time, darling," Felicia had dared, only because it was quite late, and she was in her element amidst wall-to-wall celebrities at the Rangoon Racquet Club that night. It hadn't hurt that she was giddy from the too many manhattans she'd consumed toasting the immense financial success of their latest tour.

He'd laughed at her boldness. "Is that a proposal?"

How her eyes had sparkled. She'd even hesitated, waving conspicuously at someone she knew, and he still wondered what the truthful answer to his question was.

"Don't flatter yourself," she'd replied tartly at last. "I'm not some little starlet on the make. These are the eighties in California. Besides, I seem to remember that you're not a marrying man, just as I am not a marrying woman. It's a proposition, darling. For such a sexy man, you're still so enchantingly naive."

"And old-fashioned. I always thought propositions were the man's prerogative."

"Then what's taken you so long, darling?"

"Why don't I order us another round of manhattans?"

"To stoke the fire, or to make me forget our dangerous topic of conversation?" she asked playfully when he signaled the waiter.

His eyes met hers. "I'm beginning to wonder. Felicia, you're my manager. I was taught never to mix business with pleasure."

"And I thought you were a man who made his own rules."

Only Felicia could take the upper hand with him and speak to him in that exact blend of smug conceit and affection. She had the most unendurable ego in the entertainment world, and that was saying a lot in a business clogged with insufferable egos.

Until that moment it had never occurred to him that Felicia might be interested in him in any light other than as a business property. But her eyes had been hot with that most ancient of man-woman messages, and he realized she must have been wanting him for a long time. She'd been waiting for the right time, waiting for the exact moment when he was jaded from too many shallow affairs with women who merely wanted to use him.

Felicia was the only woman who had never chased him since he'd become successful. He trusted her. He actually liked her and respected her. He'd thought about what she'd said for the rest of the night, and finally he decided maybe it was time he dated a woman with brains. It would be a change from the endless parade of bodies any other man would have envied. He'd thought perhaps that a clever woman like Felicia could bring him the inner completeness that the beauties hadn't been able to give him. It wasn't long afterward—though it was long enough to keep Felicia from believing he would ever let her dominate him—that he dropped the Vegas showgirl he'd been dating and began to escort Felicia when he needed a date.

Their first night together, he'd found that no amount of closeness with this talented and brilliant woman could banish the terrible emptiness that had shrouded his heart and soul since Gini had left him. He knew he genuinely cared for Felicia, and if he hadn't once been so vitally in love with Gini, he would probably have married Felicia. Instead he kept stalling, refusing to let her move in with him, refusing to marry her. He knew he wanted the impossible.

Jordan leaned his great, muscular body on the frail railing and stared out at Santa Monica Bay. Below, the famous beach was deserted, and the surf rolled lazily in the still moonlight. The air felt icy against his bare chest and through his thin pajama bottoms.

Damn! Why couldn't he ever sleep when he needed to? He felt too keyed up to go back to bed now. The last thing he wanted was another nightmare.

He went back inside and grabbed his guitar and began to play with a new melody while he improvised some lyrics.

"For the love of one woman, I'd start over again," crooned his low-pitched voice.

"For the love of one woman, I'd give up this life of sin.
   But I can't have her, ever again.
   So I gotta go on, living this life,
   Too many days, too many nights,
   For the love of one woman, I'd start over again...."

With a jangled thrumming of guitar strings, he broke off and sat in his silent bedroom, a look of dark torture marring his handsome features.

It was so odd that despite all the beautiful women who had thrown themselves at him over the years, despite Felicia, a stupid dream could show him that there'd never been anyone for him except one woman, Gini. Years ago, he'd realized too late what a fool he'd been to let her divorce him, and he'd gone after her to Austin. That's when her parents, the Fishers, had told him she was dead.

Jordan buried his face in his hands. Damn it! He had to find some way to put all that behind him.

But how? He was going on tour soon. He was glad suddenly. Because only when he worked really hard could he run away from the lonely feelings that made him feel he was going crazy.

The rest of that morning Jordan felt pent-up and restless, as if he were hanging on to something of vital importance by the slenderest thread. The recording session that afternoon was an abysmal failure. Nothing he or anyone else did could satisfy him. Though the band sang until they were hoarse, and squeezed moans from guitar strings until their fingers bled, the raw primal emotion in their music sounded flat to Jordan.

Everyone in the studio became tense as Jordan demanded they try again and again.

"Okay, guys, one more time," Jordan yelled. "And this time, Wolf, I don't want you to fade out on that bass."

Wolf scowled, but he nodded his shaggy head toward the others. "One more time."

Jordan began to sing, straining to express the whole range of his emotions, from sadness to raw hatred to sheer, unadulterated lust. The wild slurs and rasps in his singing, the bending of the notes, the deliberate fluctuations in rhythm and tempo evoked more feeling than anyone had ever heard in his singing, but when he finished, he cursed more terribly than before. Wolf kicked a stool aside in rage and he stood up, his great barrellike body towering over even Jordan.

"I don't know what's eating you, Jordan, but I'm through till you get yourself together," he growled roughly.

"What?"

"You heard me."

Wolf and the other members of his band stormed out of the studio, and they couldn't be induced back no matter what promises Jordan made to control his impatience.

And in Houston, Gini lay on a stretcher in a crowded emergency room, fighting for her life.

Gini moaned and opened her eyes at the faint pressure on her hand. In the brilliant light a dark, familiar face loomed close.

"Melanie," she whispered.

"Don't try to talk. You're going into surgery soon," Melanie said anxiously.

"Not much time... to say... so much."

"There's all the time in the world, Mother. You're going to be fine. The doctors all agree..."

The terrible ache sharpened in Gini's abdomen where she'd been thrown against the steering wheel. She tried to move but went white in the attempt. Something inside her felt ruptured. The sedatives she'd been given had lessened the pain, but every time she moved it was like a knife tearing her open.

"I'm going to die."

"No. Mother! You can't leave me alone."

An orderly arrived to wheel her stretcher into surgery. Gini stared wildly at her daughter.

"There's something..."

"What, Mother?"

"I have to tell you about your father."

The stark terror in Gini's voice electrified Melanie, deepening her ominous fear that her mother wouldn't survive. Melanie gripped her mother's hand fiercely. No longer did she try to make her stop talking. Instead she walked beside the stretcher, praying silently even as she listened spellbound.

"You won't be alone. Your father will take care of you."

"But I wouldn't even know where to start looking for him. There must be millions of Kings in Texas."

"No... no... not King...." Gini's voice faded into nothingness.

"What? Mother, I can't hear you."

"His name wasn't King, my darling. I know this is going to sound incredible, and I would give anything to be able to explain. But . . . now . . . there's so little time. Your father's Jordan Jacks, the singer."

"Jordan Jacks." It was like something out of a surreal fantasy. Under different circumstances Melanie wouldn't have believed her mother. But Gini continued to speak, her low voice in deadly earnest.

"If I die, you must try to reach him. Melanie, he doesn't know you even exist. He thinks I'm dead. Please . . . he may not believe you at first. It won't be an easy thing for him to accept, his having a child all these years and not knowing. You see, dear, he thought I was dead, And Melanie . . ."

"What, Mother?"

"Please . . . ask him to forgive me."

There were a thousand questions Melanie wanted to ask, but the stretcher glided relentlessly between two stainless-steel doors, and from somewhere a kind voice, said, "You can't go in there, honey."

Melanie didn't stop until a man's steel grip closed over her arms. Then she lost control, twisting and clawing like a captured wild thing.

Her poignant scream pierced the hospital quiet.

"Mother, please don't die!"

Three

It had been exactly four months, sixteen days and eleven hours since her accident. Gini knew because she'd counted every pain-filled day, this week having been the first almost normal week since the wreck.

Gini chewed the end of her red pencil and then tucked it behind her ear beneath the mass of close-cropped brown curls. Four months ago her head had been shaved for life-saving surgery.

She sat at her kitchen table, staring at the paper she had just mutilated with red scratches. She hated spending her precious Saturday afternoon grading papers, but there was no alternative. She was struggling valiantly to figure out how to word her negative reaction to Brad Clayton's theme in positive terms that would inspire him to keep trying.

She swiped the back of her hand across her perspiring brow in frustration. It was only May, but even with all the windows open and the gently droning oscillating fan that ruffled the stack of themes, the kitchen was suffocating. It was one of those terrible bright-white days so typical of a Texas spring on the Gulf Coast, the sky glaring and hazy and the intense humidity making it feel like one hundred degrees despite her cotton blouse and shorts. Her elbows kept sticking to Brad's theme. Since her accident and her prolonged convalescence, there had been no money for such luxuries as air-conditioning. She had even had to give up a car and postpone getting Melanie braces.

But it wasn't the heat and her money problems that were making it difficult for her to concentrate on her grading. It was Melanie and the unspoken battle that had been going on between them for the past four months while she'd been recuperating.

Ever since her fateful decision to tell Melanie about Jordan, Gini had known her daughter would never let the matter just drop, and she'd been dreading the inevitable confrontation. As Gini had slowly recuperated in the hospital and later at home, she'd felt Melanie's silent questions, and she'd left them unanswered. It had seemed the easiest course. She'd kept thinking, When I'm stronger, I'll be able to talk about him to her. Tomorrow I'll know what to say.

Too many tomorrows had turned into yesterdays, and she still hadn't figured out how to handle the problem.

Twenty minutes ago, when Melanie had ridden her bicycle to go buy fried chicken for their dinner, that familiar look of suppressed hostility had been in her eyes again. Melanie wasn't going to be put off much longer. Gini was actually dreading her imminent return.

This week was Gini's first back at work. The bandages on her head and the rest of her body were gone, and her hair had grown out enough to actually be flattering.

Though she was physically stronger, she still didn't feel up to dealing with Melanie on the issue of Jordan.

Gini's heart lurched at the sound of bicycle tires crunching into the shell drive outside. She looked out the window and saw Melanie pedaling her bike beneath the towering tallow trees. Melanie looked even grimmer than she had before she'd left. With growing trepidation, Gini watched her daughter throw her bike down defiantly in the tall grass beside the back door where she was never supposed to leave it. The back door banged, and Melanie stomped hurriedly across the porch before she flung the kitchen door open. Samantha, their gray cat, who wasn't allowed in, bounded inside right in front of Melanie.

"Quick, Sam, we'll have to get you to my room fast, before Mother sees you," Melanie whispered conspiratorially as she tossed a squashed cardboard box of fast-food chicken onto the kitchen counter. Her back was to her mother, and she hadn't yet seen Gini at the table.

Gini watched as Melanie flung a rolled-up piece of paper beside the box in the manner of a gauntlet being thrown down. Melanie reached inside the box and pulled out a chicken wing. Samantha stretched and extended her paws high up the cabinet door, sniffing and meowing enthusiastically. Melanie knelt to pick her cat up, but just as she did so, she saw Gini. She jumped, her young face reddening guiltily as her gaze darted back to that ominous-looking black scroll that lay beside the box of chicken. Melanie's voice, however, was steady, all pretended innocence. It was her battle voice. "Oh, hello, Mom," she said with concern and teenage nonchalance. "I thought you were resting in your bedroom."

Gini's eyes were fixed on the chicken wing that dangled so invitingly in front of Sam.

"Obviously," Gini murmured dryly.

"I was just going to put Sam out."

"You're prevaricating again, Melanie."

"And you're using English-teacher words a kid can't understand."

Definitely her battle voice, Gini decided with a sinking heart.

"Oh, you understood, all right, Put the chicken wing back, Melanie. You know we don't have money to throw away by feeding Sam our food."

Melanie obeyed. "It was only one little wing. You used to let me give her a wing when we had chicken."

"That was before we owed more than I can make for the next two years."

"I'm so tired of never having any money," Melanie lashed out. "Of you always being scared, of me never being able to do or have any of the things all the other kids have."

"I do the best I can!" Gini snapped defensively. Then she caught herself. She was running scared. She had felt desperately pushed ever since the wreck. Suddenly she realized anew the unfair burden she was placing on her child. "Go ahead and give Sam the chicken wing," she said gently. "But put her out. I don't want any more fleas."

Melanie's face brightened, and she picked Sam up to carry her outside. Gini stood up. She had to walk slowly, but after the months of therapy she could now manage short distances without a limp. She moved across the kitchen to the counter and picked up the box of chicken. "We have a couple of tomatoes. I guess I'll make a salad." Then she noticed the rolled piece of black paper again. "Hey, what's this?"

Melanie, who had returned, lunged for the poster, but she was too late. Gini was already unfurling it.

The banner waved as proudly as a flag in the breeze of the fan. The charismatic features of Jordan Jacks leaped from the black-and-yellow paper and struck Gini with the force of a thunderbolt. Her lips moved soundlessly as she read the words beneath his picture.

The poster was an advertisement for his imminent appearance at the Astrodome. Tonight he would perform a marathon four-hour set to a sellout crowd. All the proceeds were to go for medical research.

Jordan was here in Houston, and she hadn't known!

The box of chicken fell back onto the table as Gini, her face ashen with fear, somehow managed to stumble back to her chair, where she collapsed like a broken doll.

Even before Melanie said a word, Gini knew that this was the inevitable moment of confrontation she'd been dreading for four months.

The low, quiet voice came as if from a great distance. "I'm going to go hear him tonight, Mom."

"No!"

"I've got to Mom."

"I forbid it."

"You don't have that right."

"Melanie, why won't you even try to understand?"

"What is there to understand? You won't talk. For months I've waited and waited, and you've never said anything. I wanted to give you time to get better. Well, now you are. His posters are everywhere. There are ads in all the Houston newspapers. If you weren't so wrapped up in your own problems, you would have known weeks ago he was coming. Every other kid in school is going tonight. And he's my father! I want to see him. Why is that so wrong?"

"You're not going, and that's final."

"Oh, is it? For your information, I already bought the ticket with my baby-sitting money."

"You spent all that money on one ticket? Well, I don't care how you throw your money away. You're staying home tonight."

"Did he beat you or something? Are you so afraid of him because he's evil in some way, and you're afraid he'll hurt me the way he hurt you? Answer me, Mother. I want to know about my father, the good and the bad. I'm not a kid in diapers anymore. You're not the only one around here who has feelings, you know. I spent all my life thinking I didn't have a father, and then, when you're about to die in the hospital, you tell me I have a father after all, and he's really a somebody. Mom, I've read everything I can get my hands on about him since you told me, and he sounds great. But if you know he's not, I want you to tell me what he did to you that was so terrible."

As Gini's eyes misted, Melanie's tortured features blurred, and Gini buried her own face in her hands. Her head was throbbing with pain, but she knew it had nothing to do with her surgery. A leaden grief lay upon her heart. No matter how much she wanted things to be as they had been between Melanie and herself, she couldn't deliberately blacken Jordan's name to his daughter. Gini lifted her head bleakly. "He never beat me or did anything else you should be ashamed of."

The kitchen door banged shut. Gini had been speaking to an empty room. She raced out the back door as quickly as she could, which was really no more than a fast-paced hobble. She was just in time to see Melanie disappearing down the shell drive on her bike as she headed for the street.

"Melanie," Gini screamed.

Melanie just pedaled faster. She was as headstrong and stubborn as her father, Gini thought dismally, sinking down upon the back step.

Oh, why had she let it come to this? Why hadn't she summoned the courage a long time ago and talked to Melanie about her father?

Gini scarcely noticed that the jarring white glare of the afternoon had softened. The sun had emerged. There were patches of blue in the sky now. Light and shadow shimmered beneath the tall trees. A faint breeze stirred fragrant blossoms, but the new brilliance of the day did nothing to brighten the dark uncertainty in Gini's soul.

Never had Gini felt more at a loss about what she should do. Having no idea how Melanie planned to get to the rock concert, it seemed next to impossible to find her, especially since Gini no longer had a car. At last she decided to call several of Melanie's friends.

In the house, Gini dialed their numbers with fingers that trembled. Carolyn Mabry's mother said she thought maybe Melanie had gone with her daughter and a group of kids. Mr. Mabry had already left to drive them into town.

Gini called Lucy Moreno, her best friend. The phone rang six times. She was about to hang up when Lucy answered.

"Thank God you're home!" she cried frantically.

"Gini?"

"I need your help. Oh, Lucy, it's Melanie."

"I'll be right there."

It took Lucy fifteen minutes to drive over from where she lived. During that time Gini changed from her shorts into a pair of jeans. She ran a comb through her short curls and put on some lipstick. Still, when Lucy arrived she was shocked by her friend's appearance.

"Gini, you're as white as a ghost."

"You don't look like you just stepped out of *Vogue* yourself."

Lucy only laughed and smoothed her black hair, sorely in need of a haircut, out of her wide face. "I know at my weight I shouldn't wear jeans outside, but I got the impression this was an emergency. I was out raking the yard when you called."

"Oh, Lucy, I know this is probably a terrible imposition, but I've got to drive into Houston. I was hoping you'd either go with me or let me use your car. I told Melanie she couldn't go to that rock concert at the Astrodome, and she defied me. She's gone anyway."

Lucy's dark brows drew together. "That doesn't sound like Melanie. Did you two quarrel?"

Gini nodded silently. "That's all the more reason why I've got to go after her."

"Has she gone with a bad crowd?"

"I don't know who she's gone with."

"There's no way you'll ever be able to find her at the Astrodome."

"Oh, Lucy, I know that logically. But don't you see, I've got to try."

"You make it sound like life and death."

"That's the way it feels," Gini said grimly.

"Why do I have the feeling you're not telling me everything?"

"Are you coming with me or not?" Gini snapped.

"Hey. I'm your friend, remember? And I didn't mean to hit a nerve. No more questions. I'll come with you."

"What about Nick?"

"He's working tonight."

"Lucy, what would I do without you?"

"You'd be resting like you're supposed to instead of heading out on this wild goose chase."

An hour later Lucy's white Fiat was threading its way through the heavy traffic on 610 to exit at the Astrodome. It was two hours before Jordan was to go on, but the Astrodome parking lot was already jammed.

"My gosh!" Lucy cried in dismay. "Did you have any idea this place was going to be such a madhouse? Who's Melanie coming to see tonight?"

"Jordan Jacks."

In the confusion of cars, policemen, and pedestrians, it took a while to find a parking place. Gini realized that her only hope was that maybe Melanie hadn't arrived as quickly as they had. If she was already inside, there was no way they could get into the stadium without a ticket.

Lucy and Gini made their way through the parked cars and milling herds of raucous teenagers as they walked to the main entrance.

Cars overflowing with yelling kids were still pouring into the parking lot.

"So what's the plan, Gini? How do you expect to pick out your little girl in all this confusion?"

"I don't know. I—I thought I'd just stand outside the main door and hope to spot her."

Though Lucy didn't say anything, Gini felt her silent disapproval. "I know it's a long shot, Lucy."

Lucy eyed the throng of Jacks fans swarming on all sides of them. "To say the least. What if she's already inside?"

"Do you have a better idea?"

"We could go home, sit by your phone and chew our nails. Seriously, there's the greatest little Mexican restaurant on Kirby I've been dying to try."

"Lucy, you're on a diet."

"Did you have to remind me?"

Pamphlets were being distributed to the crowd by two scantily dressed girls, and the two women positioned themselves on the crates the pamphlets had been packed in. Gini stood on one side of the main entrance and looked at every long-haired boy and girl that passed them, while Lucy stood on the other side. Thirty minutes passed and there was no sign of Melanie. Gini was beginning to feel the utter futility of her plan.

Suddenly the crowd began to rave in a mindless sing-song, "Jordan we love you! Jordan we love you!"

Gini turned and saw that an immense bus was carefully threading its way through the crowd. Suddenly the bus stopped. The police looked alarmed. Four officers ran toward the giant vehicle. This was obviously an unscheduled stop.

In the last rays of the setting sun, the bus gleamed gold, and for a moment Gini was blinded.

Everything seemed to happen in slow motion. She was dimly aware of the shouts of the crowd intensifying, of the wall of people pressing closer and closer, suffocating her.

Then the doors of the bus opened.

There was a moment of the most terrible suspense.

A tall dark man stepped slowly off the bus. His black hair was illuminated in a halo of gold. His face was back-lighted, his features cast in shadow so that at first she couldn't recognize him. In the shower of sunlight spilling over him, he looked like a god. She was aware of his over-powering male charisma. She had no idea that she too was bathed in the golden light, and that to him she seemed like a translucent image from a dream.

Jordan had looked absently out of the bus and seen a flesh-and-blood replica of the vision that had haunted him day and night for over a decade. The elfin face was thinner and somehow sadder than his beloved Gini's. The cap of glossy curls was not the luxuriant brown waves he'd once buried his face in. And yet... There was something about her eyes, some unique element of gentle kindness that could belong to no other woman. A blaze of thrilling eagerness had rushed through him and propelled him out of the seat where he'd been lounging. He'd run crazily down the aisle of the bus and ordered Jake to stop.

Gini's heart shone in her eyes as she watched him walk toward her. She could feel her pulse throbbing out of control. She was filled with wild excitement, consumed by feelings she'd tried to tell herself were dead.

Never had she felt more alive.

He was striding slowly toward her, his handsome face uncertain, yet radiant with the same wild emotion that filled her. She realized suddenly that, above the chants of the fans he was calling her name.

"Gini..."

It was the most beautiful sound she had ever heard. It was a cry through time. A cry that obliterated the black years of anguish and separation. A cry that tore through all her painfully erected defenses and touched her soul.

Every sense she possessed screamed of his presence.

"Jordan...." His name was a broken whisper that was scarcely audible, but he seemed to hear her. He was mesmerized, his look of uncertainty vanishing. Abruptly he smiled that white, shy smile she had been so determined to forget but had remembered so well. Suddenly her breath caught painfully in her throat, and a violent quiver darted through her stomach.

Gini no longer heard the cries of the crowd. Time had stopped.

There was only one man and one woman.

She jumped off the box and stumbled toward him, but two stampeding teenagers shoved her roughly aside.

The crowd swarmed on top of Jordan. He was surrounded by hundreds of enthusiastic fans who dove on top of him and threw him to the ground. Gini reached toward him, and he lunged through the thickly packed herd of humanity, grabbing her slender hand in the hard, warm power of his.

At his touch, she began to tremble with the most intense emotion she'd ever felt in the whole of her life. For an instant they managed to cling to one another as if clinging to salvation, and then their fingers were torn savagely apart. Gini was thrown aside and tossed far away like a piece of flotsam on a stormy sea. Jordan yelled her name helplessly as he fought like a wild man to reach her. In the frenzy, he was tackled again and knocked to the ground. Fans fell on top of him. Some of the women began to grab pieces of Jordan's shirt and yank at his hair.

Gini began to beg. "Help him! For God's sake! Someone! They're killing him!"

Sirens whined as ten police cars hurtled toward the emergency. Dozens of officers fought their way into the crowd.

Gini was caught in the middle of the mob, and suddenly it seemed she could no longer breathe. "They're killing him," she whispered. "They're..."

Just as a police officer reached toward her, his anxious black face faded into nothingness, and she fainted in his arms, her last emotion terror for Jordan.

Gini squeezed into her seat just as the houselights dimmed and a spotlight was turned onto the stage in the middle of the Astrodome. She was so high up in the stadium, the stage looked little bigger than a postage stamp. The crowd waited with restless anticipation, and Gini was no different from the rest of them as she leaned forward in her seat, her fingernails digging into the armrest.

Oh, what craziness had prompted her to do something as preposterous as coming inside to see Jordan's show? It was just that after seeing him again, and then watching the crowd attack him, she hadn't been thinking clearly. She had merely reacted when a scalper came along with a single ticket.

She had told herself that it was only because she was afraid Jordan had been hurt, but it was more than that. She'd been filled with a longing as fierce as Melanie's to watch him, to listen to him.

Lucy had helped Gini finance the staggering price the little man had demanded. Then Lucy had driven away to have dinner at the nearby Mexican restaurant, promising Gini she would meet her in two hours in a motel lobby across the street.

Suddenly a tall, dark giant with a guitar leaped from the darkness into the circle of white light and bowed. The guitar flashed every time he moved. Sixty thousand people stood up and raved. When the uproar subsided, the honeyed resonance of Jordan's voice came over the loudspeakers, and he introduced his band.

Gini sagged against her seat, melting in relief. Jordan was all right. At least he hadn't been seriously hurt because of her; nevertheless, her heart began to pound violently.

After several jokes and a story that captivated his audience, he began to sing, and it was as if he sang only to her. She listened spellbound to one after another of his hits. First he sang "Midnight Man" and "You've Gotta Go." Others followed, the end of one song blending into the beginning of the next. She had listened to them all in secret, loving them all as she loved the man.

The curtain of warm sound enveloped her, transported her. Tears came into her eyes. What she heard was a man singing with raw emotion, a man singing from his gut, squeezing moans from his guitar strings until his fingers were raw.

His music expressed the whole range of emotions, from sadness to hatred to the most eloquent love. He threw the full force of his being into his singing. The husky slurs of his voice, the bending of notes, the deliberate fluctuations in tempo and rhythm, all these were blues techniques calculated to unleash emotions, and unleash them they did. The crowd's response was electric.

There was an honesty in his lyrics, a deep underlying integrity, a power that reached out and touched everyone who listened. There were no fancy light shows, no special effects, no outrageous costumes and no bizarre acts performed on stage.

Jordan just gave his all to his music, and the effect was overpowering. As his throaty voice caressed her, goose bumps pricked her arms. She wanted to weep, yet her emotion was too profound for tears. He gave pleasure because he found pleasure in his music, and his fans loved him for it. They listened as she did, enraptured.

There were people of every age and description in the audience, and Gini had been surprised to realize that they weren't all teenagers. His appeal was broader than that.

He began to sing the one song she had never been able to listen to. She heard her name resounding in the vast stadium, "Gini...Gini...Gini..." and never had his voice rung with more soul-searching sadness. She remembered their hands being torn apart in the parking lot. In that moment she had forgotten he was a star. She'd seen him only as a man she loved.

"In every stranger's face I still search for you...."

She felt his profound loss because it was hers as well. Through the years she had longed for him too. Suddenly it was more than she could bear. By coming to his show she had relearned what she had always known. Jordan could never belong to her. He belonged to his art, to his music. He belonged to the world.

She got up and stumbled blindly down the aisle to the nearest exit.

Four

Outside, the muffled sound of thousands of chanting fans could be heard.

Jordan was slumped against the wall. His black hair that fell over his brow was wringing wet with perspiration, his white shirt soaked through. He took the towel that dangled from his wide shoulders and mopped his bronzed face and brow again, careful not to press too hard beneath his right eye or against the dark bruises on his cheek that showed through the Pan-Cake makeup Felicia had forced him to apply before he went on stage.

From across the room his drummer, Louie, shouted above the din in the crowded dressing room. "That was one helluva performance. You were great, boss, black eye and all."

Jordan smiled faintly in response. "Maybe I sing better when I feel like I'm dying."

"You're lucky you weren't killed," Felicia whispered furiously into his ear as she handed him a beer.

All evening Felicia had been hovering much too possessively to suit Jordan. "Better not have a beer, Felicia. You know what the doctor said. But I'll take another glass of water."

Felicia returned with a tall glass of ice water.

"What got into you to stop the bus and get off like that, Jordan?" she demanded.

Jordan merely glared at Felicia. He knew better than to mention Gini to her. That was the one subject they had never been able to talk about.

"If only I hadn't been tied up by the press," Felicia was saying, "I would have been with you, darling, and I could have stopped you from doing something that was so incredibly foolhardy. You're lucky you got by with a few bruises and the possibility of a couple of broken ribs. You need to shower so we can run you by that hospital and have those X rays the doctor ordered. I hated to see you performing when the doctor told you not to."

"The night I don't go on when people are counting on me, I'd better be dead," Jordan said grimly.

"You could have seriously jeopardized your health."

Though he knew it was unfair of him, Felicia's passionate show of concern tonight was putting him on edge. All he wanted was to be left alone so that he could think, but she kept hovering. It was as if she sensed that her place in his affections was threatened.

"I made it, didn't I?" he snapped. All night he'd kept thinking of Gini. Had the girl he'd seen been real or a figment of his imagination? He was always nervous before a performance. Had his nerves been playing tricks on him? If she was real, was there some way he could find her?

"Jordan, what is it? Something's eating at you. I can feel it."

"It's not something I can talk about. Okay?"

"Okay," she said, "for now."

"Why don't you make sure everybody stays happy while I shower," he said, forcing warmth into his voice in a deliberate attempt to soothe the feathers he had ruffled. He leaned down and kissed the top of her head. "Felicia, don't worry. My black mood has nothing to do with you."

She nodded unhappily. She was too strong-minded to be easily placated.

Jordan was about to leave when he became aware of a commotion at the outer door in the next room. Louie was out there talking to someone. An overly eager fan, no doubt, who was determined to see him. The last thing Jordan wanted tonight was further contact with zealous fans, yet some instinct made him put off his shower and stay to find out what was going on.

Louie came up to him a few minutes later, a crumpled note in his hand.

Childish scrawl in black felt tip leaped from a fringed sheet of notebook paper.

"Please believe this! I really am your daughter, and I have to see you! Just this once!" The note was signed Melanie King.

"This has gotta be the craziest night we ever played," Louie was saying. "Boss, I know this is going to sound weird, but this kid actually does kind of look..."

Wolf, who had overheard, said, "Jordan, this is just another of those fraudulent paternity raps. Every kid in America wants to be a princess with a millionaire daddy."

"You're probably right, Wolf," Jordan murmured, "but what were you going to say, Louie?"

"She kind of takes after you, boss. She's got black hair. And..."

"Hell," Wolf said, "half the kids in this country have black hair. She's probably been looking in the mirror every morning for a year, figuring out ways to make herself look more like Jordan."

"Maybe I should see her," Jordan said.

"If you do that, and she's a crazy, it might be hours before we get rid of her," Wolf argued. "There's no telling what she might do or say. What if it makes the papers? Let Felicia handle it."

Jordan hesitated briefly before relenting. "You're right, of course."

Armed with the tattered note, her face a steel mask, Felicia walked briskly into the adjoining room. Jordan almost felt sorry for any kid who had to go up against Felicia.

He went to the door, opened it a fraction of an inch, and listened. He heard a young, quavering voice that he had never heard before, and yet it moved him in some unfathomable way.

"You don't understand, Miss Brenner. I'm not some kook. Mr. Jacks really is my father."

"Where in the world did you ever come up with such a far-fetched idea as that?" Felicia demanded.

"My mother told me he was."

"Oh, I see," Felicia said carefully, letting her nasty-nice tone imply something quite unpleasant.

"No! You don't!" The young voice had become passionate.

"My mother's not like that! She's a schoolteacher, and she didn't want me to come here tonight. She only told me the truth about my father because she nearly died four months ago. She's been very sick for a long time."

"Look, this story is getting wilder and wilder. You need money, am I right? To pay all the hospital bills? I know you want to help your mother, but you've got to understand that whatever your problems are, they're certainly not Mr. Jacks's responsibility. You look like a nice kid. Not the kind to try to slap some far-out paternity suit on a rock star."

"You won't even listen to me, will you? I think you're afraid to let me talk to him."

"I'm not afraid of you, little girl. I've been through this a million times with people whose stories were a lot slicker than yours. You're never going to make this stick."

"I just want to see him for five minutes."

At that Jordan pushed the door open and stepped inside. "I'll handle things from here, Felicia," he said ever-so-softly, yet his voice held the tone of command.

Felicia's eyes were bright and hard. "I really don't think that's very wise, Jordan."

He scarcely heard what she said. Outside, coming from a great distance somewhere in the Astrodome, the sing-song ravings of his fans went on. But in the tiny room there was a silence so profound it seemed that no one even breathed.

Jordan was aware of his blood pounding against his eardrums, of a cold fright, quickly followed by a terrible joy. His entire attention was transfixed as he stared at the young girl Felicia had been talking to, and he realized that she was his.

For a long moment he stood perfectly still, letting the rush of blood and excitement subside a little.

She was his! This black-haired bean pole in the skin-tight jeans and oversized hot-pink T-shirt, this rebellious-looking woman-child with the huge dark eyes and slightly crooked teeth was his! The roar in his ears came again.

It was as if he had turned back a page of time and seen himself at the same age.

He was shocked by the intensity of his elation, baffled not so much by the sense of the unreal as by his thrilling happiness. Suddenly his world held the promise of something very bright, something he had long ago despaired of ever possessing, and he was determined that, no matter what he had to do, no matter what it cost him, he would not let it slip away.

It was not a coincidence that that woman had been outside the Astrodome. He felt almost sure this child was connected to her in some way.

His bronzed features were unreadable, his outward manner betraying none of his inner excitement.

The girl who stood before him was remarkable because she was a feminine version of the thirteen-year-old he had been. In a glance Jordan took in her sulky coltishness, her stubborn defiance as well as the painful uncertainty of her youth. Just as he had been then, she was filled with conflicting adolescent urges. She had fought her way in to see him, yet instead of happiness at this success, her expression now showed hostile confusion. She looked like she was wondering if she hadn't gotten herself in too deep this time. This girl, who had talked her way past the ranks of police outside, who had defeated Felicia, now stood before him and stared at him speechlessly.

Jordan was only vaguely conscious of the voices in the background. He was too fascinated by this startling replica of himself.

"Nice-looking kid," Louie was saying.

"Same story though, Louie. For all her apple-pie sweetness, what do you bet all she wants is money?"

"Or her picture in the newspaper. Everybody wants a piece of the boss."

"That's the one thing that never changes," Felicia finished cynically.

Melanie, who had been listening, cried in horror, "You're wrong. All of you! I don't want any money." Her young face was wild with hurt. She turned the full force of her feelings on Jordan. "And you're not my father. I don't want you to be my father! Mother was right about you when she told me to stay away from you!"

With that outburst Melanie would have turned on her heels and vanished from his life forever had not Jordan lunged in front of her. The quick movement wrenched his rib cage, and he went white as he gave a yelp of pain. Despite his injured ribs, he caught her at the door. When she began frantically twisting the knob, his brown hand covered hers.

She flinched as though burned, and he pulled his hand from hers. "I won't touch you," he said gently. "If you won't run away."

"I don't want money," she whispered raggedly.

"I believe you."

"You're the first person around here who does, then."

He smiled. "What do you want?"

Her black eyes flashed. "I just wanted to see you. And now that I have, I want to go home."

His stomach knotted at her eagerness to escape him. He fought to make his voice light. "Obviously you don't think I'm much to look at. Look, I couldn't help that I got slugged in the eye tonight. I know I need a shower, but when I make the effort, I'm not that terrible looking."

"Oh, it's not just your looks."

Again there was that pull in his stomach that had nothing to do with his injuries. This was his kid, and he hadn't the slightest notion of how to talk to her. What could he do or say to make her stay? Suddenly, because he felt the need

to vent his frustration on someone, Jordan turned on Felicia, Louie and Wolf, who were watching them with an
avid, speculative interest, and barked sharply, "Why don't
you let us have a few minutes alone, okay? And don't let
anyone else in here for a while."

When they had gone, Jordan turned back to Melanie.
"Do you suppose we could sit down? As I said, I got kind
of roughed up before I went on tonight."

She nodded, and he led her to the couch. They sat at
either end, facing each other warily. She sat rigidly as
though she were very ill at ease. Jordan's great body was
sprawled negligently, but it was a pretense at negligence.

"You said I was your father." Was that halting, unsure
voice really his? Never in all of his life had he felt more
self-conscious.

The defiance came back into her face. Dark eyes blazed.
"I was wrong."

"What changed your mind?"

"I don't want a father like you."

He didn't know whether to laugh or cry. In the end he
threw back his head and laughed, and this did a great deal
to break the tension between them. "I don't blame you.
What kind of father would you prefer?"

"I never had a father, or at least I never thought I had.
So I used to imagine I had one. He was always the kind of
guy that would do things with a kid. He would go to my
piano recitals, take me fishing, or help me with my homework. He wouldn't make fun of me when I played the
guitar. He was just . . . ordinary. Not some god."

"I'm not some god."

"You wouldn't have time for a kid."

"If I had a daughter as beautiful as you, I would make
time," he said gravely.

"You're famous. You have too many more important things to do."

"Nothing would be more important than my child."

A look of the most profound yearning had come into Melanie's eyes. And there was fury, too—fury because she so desperately craved a father's love, fury at him because she'd never had it.

Jordan said, "A long time ago I was married to a woman I loved. Her name was Gini."

A little cry of pain erupted from Melanie's trembling lips. "That's my mother's name. You really are... Damn you! Why did you walk out on her? On us? Why didn't you take us with you?"

A chill went through Jordan. "Is that what she told you?"

"She never told me anything."

"She was the one who left."

"I don't believe you! You probably thought she wasn't good enough for you."

"I'm beginning to see why your mother doesn't talk to you. Do you want to hear what I have to say, or not?"

Melanie shrugged her thin shoulders. "Okay, so I want to hear."

"When I started to become a star, Gini gave me my freedom. She said she didn't want to stand in my way, that she couldn't get along in the music world and would hold me back. That was over thirteen years ago. I had no idea she was expecting a child, or I would never have let her go. I was a fool to have done it in any case, because I never got over her. Tonight I saw a woman in the parking lot that reminded me of her. I stopped the bus, but when I tried to reach her, my fans went crazy. We were both trampled."

"She must have come after me to stop me from seeing you."

"Tell me something." He leaned forward. He was aware of his pulse beginning to pound wildly in his temples. "There's something I have to know. Is your mother married or in love with anyone else?"

There was a long moment of awful suspense while his soul hung in jeopardy.

"She never dates anybody," Melanie answered at last.

Relief washed through Jordan. "I want you to give me her telephone number. I'm going to call her and tell her you're all right and that I'm bringing you home myself."

"You can't do that! She'll kill me!" Melanie cried.

"I don't think so. Your mother would never intentionally hurt anyone."

"You're not her kid. You don't know her like I do."

"I'll be there to protect you."

She leaned forward and reached tentatively for his hand. When she touched him, he gripped hers fiercely.

"Maybe you're not the guy I dreamed about," she said hesitantly. "But maybe you'll be okay."

"Oh, Melanie. Honey."

She let him fold her into his arms.

"Remember. I only said maybe," she whispered, hugging him tightly. "And you do need a shower something terrible."

Then she began to weep. "I shouldn't have said that, should I? It's just that I don't know what to say to you."

"You can say anything you like, Melanie. Anything at all."

Because he wanted privacy when he talked to Gini, Jordan had decided to hold off calling her until they left the confusion of the Astrodome and got to his hotel. He had rented the entire top floor of one of the most luxurious hotels in Houston. Melanie had taken one of his guitars into the next room and was playing it for Wolf and Louie, who were now completely enchanted by her. The minute she had picked up Jordan's guitar, struck the first note and begun to sing, they had declared that they no longer doubted she was his child. She was, they said, a natural, like her father.

Not Felicia.

"You're a fool to let yourself be hoodwinked by that kid, Jordan," Felicia blazed. "A damned fool! Worse than that, since now you won't let me take you to the hospital. You could be bleeding inside."

"I know what you think, and I appreciate your concern. But right now, if you don't mind, I'd like a little privacy. I want to call her mother."

"And you want me to leave, I take it?"

He glanced toward her wearily. "Is that really so much to ask? You have your own suite. I'm dead tired, and I've got to drive Melanie home."

"You don't have to go yourself. You could have Jake—"

"I promised Melanie." His voice was as hard as steel.

"Then I'll go with you."

"No."

"You've really taken this father thing to heart, haven't you? You're not even sure she's your kid."

"I'm sure."

Something in his hard look made her realize she'd better back off. "Oh, all right! I'm going." She picked up her purse and slung it angrily over her shoulder.

When he was sure she had gone and wouldn't return, Jordan walked into his bedroom, locked the door and picked up the phone. Gini answered on the third ring.

"Hello."

The soft sound of her uncertain voice was no more than the gentlest caress, but it set him on fire. His fingers clenched the phone, and he almost hated her for the power she had to bring him to his knees. And after thirteen years.

"This is Jordan," he said quietly. He sank down onto the bed, despising himself for the intensity of his feelings. She had walked out on him. She had had her parents lie to him about her death. And he was such a fool, he still wanted her.

"Oh, my God," she murmured. The joyless note of doom in her low tone jarred agonizingly through his nervous system.

"That really was you at the Astrodome, wasn't it?" he demanded on a raw note of agony, remembering how terribly he had fought to reach her.

"Yes."

"You're okay then?" He could not stop his voice from gentling.

"I'm okay." she whispered. "But what about you? I thought they were going to kill you."

"Believe me, it felt like they were trying. I have a few bruises," he confessed, minimizing his injuries. Then his anger drove him to say, "As if you really care."

After the briefest hesitation, she said faintly, "I care, Jordan."

He felt a stab of jealous anger that those three words, words that were probably nothing more than an effort on her part to be polite, could matter to him so much.

"All these years, you let me believe you were dead," he rasped.

"Yes."

"Damn it!" he cried with grim pain. "Is that all you can say?"

"Jordan, I—I thought it was for the best."

"You obviously thought keeping Melanie from me was for the best, too," he ground out, bitter sarcasm coating his words.

"Yes."

"How could you do that? All these years I grieved for you. How would you have felt if you'd believed *I* was dead? If I'd kept your only child from you?"

"Jordan, I..." Her voice was taut as though to keep out tremors. She broke off, so upset she couldn't answer him.

He heard the catch in her voice, the tiny involuntary shudder, and he forced himself to halt his anger. "I just wanted you to know Melanie's all right," he said in a softer tone that veiled his powerful, uncontrollable emotions. "She's here, with me at my hotel right now. I'll be bringing her home in an hour or so."

"Jordan, maybe it would be better if you didn't come yourself."

"Better for whom: you?" he declared in a contemptuous breath, the full force of his smoldering anger returning because she was rejecting him.

"For all of us. Melanie and I are a family now. There's no place in our life for you."

"No place..." His stomach tightened into a hard ball of pain as he realized how determined she was to keep him out of their lives.

"You listen to me, Gini Jacks," he muttered in a thick, strange voice that wasn't his own at all. "And that last is still your name whether or not you claim it. I'm back in your life even if you don't want me to be. You kept my daughter from me. You've had your way for thirteen damn years. Now I'm going to have mine."

He slammed the phone down before she could say anything else that would rip him apart. Confusion was tearing at him. So, she didn't want him disturbing the cozy life she had made for herself. That hurt. But when he thought of the chaos and unreality of his life he didn't blame her. How could he take her or Melanie on tour? Was he suddenly to simply give up his career? To tell everyone who depended on him their jobs were over? Music was his life, his soul. And yet, so was Gini and their daughter. He hadn't the vaguest idea what the solution was. He only knew that the emptiness he had felt all these years, believing Gini dead, had vanished now that he knew she was alive and they had a daughter. He was determined to win his wife back.

Five

It was two o'clock in the morning when Jordan's limousine braked silently beneath the darkness of the trees in front of Gini's house. A humid breeze stirred the branches and made the leaves high above rustle like dry papers. Against the horizon, lightning whitened the blackness of the sky, and thunder rumbled. Melanie had fallen asleep, and her head lay against her father's shoulder as naturally as if they'd known each other for her entire lifetime instead of just a few hours of it.

With a renewal of his grim resolve, Jordan stared at the brightly lit house nestled beneath the sheltering trees. It looked as if Gini were burning every light in anticipation of his visit. His gaze returned to his child. Though he hated to wake her, he nudged Melanie gently. She stirred in his arms, her dark eyes fluttering open.

When she saw him, she smiled drowsily. "So you're not a dream," she mused.

He noted with pleasure that she made no effort to remove her head from his shoulder. "No. I'm not a dream," he replied in his gentlest tone.

"You seem like one."

"Not for long," he murmured dryly as he helped her from the car and led her up the sidewalk.

In a glance he took in the ankle-length grass, the boards on the house that were peeling from lack of paint and the torn front screens on the windows and door. So, this was the paradise Gini was so determined to exclude him from.

"Careful," Melanie cautioned. "The third step is sort of rotten. We never use the front door, you see."

"I see," he said coolly as he stepped over the black board.

Melanie took out her key and unlocked the front door.

"You're coming inside to help me with Mother, remember?"

"Oh, I remember."

She led him into their homey living room. He stood in the center of it, dominating it with his restless male presence. Despite the simplicity of the furnishings, they were comfortable. It was the kind of room where a man could prop his feet up without worrying about hurting anything. There was a warmth and charm that was lacking both in his lavish Malibu palace and in the luxurious hotel suites he'd grown accustomed to.

His eyes ran over the plump couch Gini had discovered in a little shop outside Galveston for twenty-five dollars and reupholstered. It was swaddled in two cheery afghans that Gini had knitted herself. There were handwoven baskets stacked on shelves, pots overflowing with lush green plants, and hand-painted ladder-back chairs. All the items in the room were unique, as if they were orphans Gini had found in junk shops and garage sales and decoratively arranged so that they now got on as family. On the wall hung a series of photographs of Melanie. An awful looking gray cat, no doubt an adored pet, sat in a window and regarded him warily through narrowed eyes, tail twitching. Jordan realized it had been a lifetime since he'd been inside a real home.

Suddenly feeling ill at ease, Jordan began to adjust his tie. When he had finished, the damn thing felt even tighter than before. He rarely wore a suit, and his body felt imprisoned by the tight collar at his throat, and the scratchy cuffs at his wrists. Because of the extra layers of clothing, he was immediately aware of the heat and humidity in the house. It felt as if he'd stepped inside a sauna. He let his hands fall to his sides, where he clenched them against his thighs impatiently.

Then he saw her.

Gini was standing like a frozen statue in the shadowy doorway that led to the dining room. She wore the rich, flowing scarlet caftan that Lucy had given her when she was well enough to quit wearing hospital gowns. For all her attempt to dissuade him from coming, Jordan realized the caftan was an attempt at glamour. The soft material clung to her body. She had wanted to be beautiful for him.

"Hello, Mother," Melanie said nervously. "You look pretty tonight."

"I think you'd better go to your room, young lady," Gini managed in an ominously low voice. "I'll deal with you later."

Melanie glanced conspiratorially at her father before obeying, only to feel disappointment that he was no longer looking at her. He was staring at her mother, who seemed suddenly to be clutching the doorframe for support.

Gini's brown hair was tousled, loose tendrils of it falling against her rosily flushed cheeks, her breasts heaving with exertion as if she'd heard them outside and rushed headlong through the house, only to stop when the front door opened and Jordan had stepped inside.

Gini lifted her gaze to his.

There was a dreamlike unreality to the moment.

In her eyes he read intense emotion.

The floor felt unsteady beneath his feet as he devoured her with his gaze.

"I asked you not to come," she whispered brokenly.

Her words cut through him like a sharp blade, but he masked his feelings. "I had to talk to you."

"You must be losing your touch. Couldn't you find some other woman to force yourself on?"

There was a slashing curve to his mouth, a cynical smile. His voice gentled dangerously. "I wasn't looking for one, Gini. You dressed up tonight—for me. Perhaps you're not as sorry I'm here as you pretend," he said quietly. "Now are you?"

She made a low, strangled sound as though she wished she could deny what he'd said. She tore her eyes from his.

"I see. So you're determined to hate me?"

It seemed a lifetime before she answered.

"I could never hate you, Jordan. I just want you out of my life."

"I won't go along with that anymore," he said grimly. Jordan started toward her, opening his arms. Gini hesitated, her lovely face twisted with tortured conflict, and then she covered the short distance that separated them, flying into his open arms. Jordan enfolded her in a crushing embrace that made him aware of every damaged rib.

"I'm so mixed-up, Jordan," she murmured. "I want you to go, and yet..."

He held her tightly, burying his face in her hair, taking in the smell of her, the scent and feel of her clean, silken curls and her sweet, warm flesh, the exquisite sensation of her velvet body melting into his.

This was the fantasy that had filled his dreams. But this was real. She was real. Even if she didn't want him, at least she wasn't dead. The grim specter that had cloaked his life with despair through the years was illusion. He was too happy she was alive for anger.

"It's been so long. A lifetime," he murmured against her hair in an odd, tight voice. "I never intend to do without you again."

As Gini listened to him and held on to him, she was unable to give him all her carefully planned arguments to talk him into leaving. She had known loneliness so long. The intoxicating pleasure of having him again, even for a few hours, was too great. She clung to him. She was lost to the world as he held her, lost to the rightness or wrongness of their relationship, lost to everything except that she was starving for him. At least for this moment she didn't care if they came from two different worlds. All she wanted was to give in to the thrilling happiness of having him once more. In a few minutes she would regain her perspective and be able to fight him.

For him the world was filled with hope again.

Gently Jordan brushed Gini's lips with his. At the first touch of her trembling mouth, his arms tightened convulsively upon her shoulders. He pressed her slender curves against the hard contours of his body, their kiss having unleashed a storm of male passion.

"I've lived in hell since you left me, Gini," he whispered hoarsely as his tongue ravished her mouth, entering it and touching her tongue deliberately. She was as sweet as honey. "I never stopped loving you. No one, nothing has ever filled the emptiness in my heart."

His mouth had moved lower and was nuzzling the side of her neck, his lips circling erotically.

"Jordan. Oh, Jordan... I'm supposed to be telling you to go. And just look at me." Her low tone quivered with fervent longing.

Her body arched into his, and he felt the completeness of her breathless response. She was soft and pliant in his arms. She drove him wild. He stroked her softly with his roughened hand. It was as if he'd never had a woman in all the years they'd been apart.

"If you really love me, you'll walk out of here tonight and forget me," she murmured helplessly, gasping back a sob.

"I don't understand that kind of love, Gini," he said, drawing her even more closely inside the steel circle of his hands. "I need you. I ache for you. That's what love means to me. I've lived without you too long to let you go now that I've found you again."

"You've never known what it is to be afraid, Jordan."

"You're so wrong. I'm afraid now. Afraid that somehow I'll lose you all over again."

He broke off, his desire sweeping him. He moved with deliberate slowness, pressing her body against the wall, making her feel his power over her, making her know the response that built up in him at her slightest touch. Making her know how much he wanted her.

"For thirteen hellish years I thought you were dead," he said with fevered passion, "and part of me was dead as well." His hand traced the velvet softness of her throat lovingly. "Now I find you alive. How many men ever get a second chance like that? For thirteen years I've said, 'if only Gini were alive, everything would be different.' How many if-onlys ever come true? This is the stuff of dreams, my love. Of miracles. Only a fool would walk away."

She began to tremble, her dark eyes luminous with unshed tears. Through the years she'd had a few if-onlys of her own. Her fingers reached up to caress the dark bruises that marred the perfection of his bronzed handsomeness. "This afternoon you were hurt...because of me," she said.

He caught her hand and brought it to his lips. She felt the hot imprint of his mouth, first burning between the insides of her fingers and then upon the back of her slim wrist, where her pulse had begun to race chaotically beneath his lips. She shivered.

"When I saw you standing out there in that ocean of teenagers, Gini, I never thought what might happen. I only thought of you. I would have braved hell itself to find you again."

"You could have been killed."

"We must celebrate the fact I was not," he said, his voice going husky with desire. His lips curved into his famous rakish grin, devastating the last remnants of her flimsy emotional control.

"We must have nothing more to do with one another," she whispered.

"You're crazy." His brilliant eyes were blatantly sensual.

He lowered his lips and kissed her passionately. His warm male smell filled her nostrils, heightening her awareness of him.

Her hands slid hesitantly beneath his coat, over his crisp shirt. The hard feel of his flesh beneath her exploring hands rocked her senses. The warmth of his breath blew against her upturned cheek. She caught the heady scent of his cologne.

"I want to spend the night," he said with rough urgency. His fingers caressed the lush softness of her full breast.

"No. Besides, what would Melanie think if you're here in the morning?"

His mouth blew a hot, scorching kiss through scarlet material onto the tip of her nipple. He glanced upward into her desire-darkened eyes in time to see her shudder. "She'll think her mother and father are in love."

"Won't that be giving her false hope?"

He was determined to bind her to him in any way he could. Even if it meant using their child. "Not as far as I'm concerned." He knelt to cherish the other breast with the same sweet warmth he'd shown its twin.

"Oh, Jordan, I can't let you stay," she moaned.

"You can't make me go."

His hands began to undo her caftan, and she didn't even try to stop him. The bright red fabric parted, and she shivered when she felt the heat of his fingers upon her naked skin. It was so easy to give in to him. So hard to fight him. "You're mine," he said. "You always have been. And you always will be."

"Please let me go."

"No, love," he murmured softly, kissing her. "Never again will I be without you." He lifted her into his arms and carried her across the living room. Ignoring her protests, he lowered her onto the soft couch and began undressing her, all the time murmuring empassioned endearments, kissing her lips, stilling her fears with gentle caresses. At last she closed her eyes and lay still, the intimate touch of his hands and the low throb of his voice having mesmerized her.

"I can't fight you any longer," she admitted in defeat.

He pulled her caftan from her shoulders, his eyes travelling slowly over her voluptuously swelling breasts, down to her slender hips. When he saw the two scars across her stomach, he knelt and kissed them. "Melanie told me about the accident, that you nearly died."

"I have more stitches than Frankenstein's monster."

"You're even more beautiful than ever."

"You could have anybody."

"I only want you."

She had never believed that. Her hands played in the raven thickness of his hair. "So many people are enthralled by you. You're like a god."

That was the second time he'd heard that tonight.

"I'm a man," he said fiercely. Something wild and frightening had come into his voice. "Not a god. Those people who think that are in love with an image, not a human being. You've got to stop thinking like them. Do you think they would have tried to tear me to pieces this afternoon if I was real to them? No, Gini, I'm just a man. That's all I've ever been. And like any man, I need one woman who really loves me. You never tried to use me, Gini. I know you never will. A man in my position can't know that about very many people. Real love is an infinitely precious possession, and fame only makes it all the harder to have."

"I can't fit into your world."

He kissed her again and pushed the tousled, gleaming brown curls back from her forehead, gently cradling her in his arms, but she felt the terrible tension that hardened every muscle in his body. "How do you know, when you've never tried?"

"Jordan..."

"Promise me you won't leave me without at least trying."

She sensed his desperation. She remembered the haunting words of the song he'd written about her. Perhaps she had been wrong thirteen years ago. Perhaps he really did need her. Perhaps she really had hurt him terribly. But it didn't matter. She couldn't let it matter.

"I can't promise you."

"Then I'll have to force you."

"How?"

"There's Melanie. You won't deny her the chance to have a father, will you?"

"Jordan, that's not fair."

"What is fair, Gini?" he demanded, his low voice raw with pain. "Was it fair of you to haunt me for thirteen years? I have no intention of playing fair. The stakes are too high. And I have no intention of losing when the bounty is you."

"Jordan, no..." Frantically she fought to push him away.

"Tonight I intend to find out if the fire in my soul is for a ghost or a woman."

Six

___

This is wrong, Jordan," Gini pleaded one last, useless time.

The silent night surrounded them, and out of the hushed black silence came his voice, low and demanding.

"That's what you keep telling me, but I'll never believe it. You belong to me, Gini. Tonight is our new beginning."

He was gripping her so tightly that her arms were aching. She clawed in a vain attempt to escape him.

"I hate your caveman approach," Gini said desperately.

"Then I'll be gentle, love," he whispered as she tried to twist away.

His hand ran ever so lightly over her as he touched her with a startling, mind-shattering gentleness that caught them both by surprise.

She gasped. A tremor of wild rapture stole through her. "That wasn't what I meant." She was caught between her desire for him and her will to resist.

"Wasn't it? You seem to be enjoying it though," he taunted before his mouth claimed hers once more.

This time his lips assaulted her mouth with unrestrained passion. His kisses took her breath away and drained the strength from her body, leaving her limp in his arms. His thirst for her wasn't quenched by simple surrender. He plundered the sweetness of her mouth again and again.

Only when her fingers curled weakly around his neck did he ease the pressure of his mouth on hers to masterful possession. Only when he knew she was his.

She began to tremble with desire. She couldn't fight his male attraction any more than she could fight the wild ecstasy his lovemaking aroused.

His lips were torture and bliss combined, and Gini hated herself for responding.

Against her earlobe his voice was low and brutal. "You're mine, now and for always."

Jordan lifted her into his arms and carried her through the house, searching for her bedroom. Her head was crushed against his chest, and she could hear the furious pounding of his heart beneath her ears. She was afraid, yet she was on fire with an emotion more powerful than fear.

The house was whirling black darkness, and he was darkness, and in this mad, all-consuming darkness they were one. When he reached her bedroom door, she felt wild with terror. Suddenly she knew that if she didn't fight him now, she would never be able to.

She started to scream, but his lips closed over hers, muffling her cry, his hard kiss ruthlessly erasing everything from her mind but her awareness of him.

Lightning blazed against the windows, and outside the world resounded with thunder. A fierce wind had come up, and the house trembled beneath its blasts. Or was it he who was shaking so fiercely?

His lips traveled downward, over her throat, between her breasts, where they burned against soft, naked flesh. Very gently he kissed each terrible scar. He was whispering love words, unintelligible sweet things that he'd never said to her before.

"Tell me you want me, Gini," he demanded roughly at last. When she made no answer, the husky command came again, more insistent than before. "Tell me, Gini."

Through blurred eyes of desire, she studied the brown male face so near her own. His expression was both violent agony and soul-destroying love.

"I want you," she admitted faintly.

Her whispered words stole his wrath, and he smiled down at her tenderly, that shy half smile she had always loved. With his smile he wove a spell that turned back the pages of time. The years between them were gone. They were young and in love. A glowing heat flowed in her veins.

He kissed her again, more sweetly than before. Then he carried her inside and slowly lowered her to the bed. He stood up once more while she lay upon the bed, her body aflame with sensual longings.

Her eyes followed him everywhere. He went to the windows and drew the blinds. Then he came back to the bed, where he towered over her, his legs thrust widely apart, his stance primitive and conquering.

Her luminous golden-brown eyes locked with the brilliant dark fire of his. Without a word he began to undress, and Gini watched him with unashamed eyes, marveling at the masculine perfection of his body. Somewhere in the back of her mind she was dimly aware that she should get up and run, but it was too late for that. She was too filled with the warm flood of sensations his hard kisses had aroused.

He unknotted his tie and ripped it from his neck. Then came his coat, his shirt and the rest of his clothes. With them he shed the last vestiges of civilization. He was sleek and brown, as powerfully built as a jaguar, only more beautiful. Much more beautiful, she thought weakly as a pagan shiver fluttered through her, and she lowered her lashes so he could not see how deeply his obvious state of male arousal affected her.

He came toward her, and her senses reeled as he brought his naked torso down to hers. Her hardened nipples mashed into the bristly black hairs of his chest. Briefly, because of his bruised rib cage, he winced. But only briefly. His desire for her immediately overcame the slight pain of his injuries.

Then it was heated flesh against heated flesh, male against female, and all the differences and the years that had divided them were gone. They were simply two people who wanted each other too much to deny themselves.

They were silent. Intense. Enraptured. Their bodies seeking. Needing. Hot lips burned intimate kisses on damp satin skin. Then his mouth searched out the frantic pulse at her throat and lingered there. Slowly his hands moved over her arms, her waist, down the creaminess of her thighs, before his legs gently forced her legs apart.

Almost in slow motion her body arched to accept his fevered maleness. With infinite gentleness he took her, his thighs at last coming to rest intimately against her soft warm flesh. Only after he'd given her time to grow accustomed to him did he begin to move, slowly at first, and then more fiercely.

A trembling weakness spread throughout Gini's body, making her a willing slave to his ardent lovemaking.

"Jordan." His name was a moan of pleasure, and he brought his mouth to kiss the source that called to him.

Her arms circled his neck and trailed over the hard muscles of his shoulders and back, moist with the beads of passion. He shuddered from her slightest touch.

His breathing was deep and ragged, and she realized he was as ravaged by desire as she.

Suddenly she felt she was fainting, and yet at the same time she felt brilliantly alive.

He held her tightly, their bodies melting one into the other as their passion carried them to heights neither had ever reached before. For an instant two souls merged into one on the flame of mutual surrender.

Without a word, Jordan held her against his body as their passion subsided. She was aware of their heartbeats thundering in unison.

What had happened between them was too wonderful for words. But even in that moment of shared ecstasy there was pain. She couldn't let passion change anything between them. Their relationship had always been impossible, and it still was. More so than ever. Tomorrow, she thought unhappily. I'll have to talk him into letting me go tomorrow. Tomorrow—when we can both think rationally.

That night he woke her again and again to make love to her. It was as if having had her once, he only wanted her all the more. At last, just before the sun came up, he allowed her to sink into a deep and dreamless sleep.

The next morning she was the first to awaken. The house was eerily quiet, though she knew it must be late. That could only mean Melanie hadn't gotten up yet either.

Outside, raindrops dripped from the trees. A mocking-bird fussed excitedly. Probably Samantha was on the prowl.

Gini lay in the semidarkness, her mind a chaotic whirl of half-remembered sensuality.

Oh, the hot, dark, shameless splendor Gini felt as she realized that, no matter how she'd tried to deny it, she was still a woman. Jordan's woman.

The velvet-black night and the hours of lovemaking they'd shared had passed like a sensuous dream, but they had left her with the knowledge that no matter how she'd tried to pretend otherwise, she'd never stopped loving Jordan. Again he had possessed her body; he'd always possessed her heart and mind.

Curled sleepily against the hard warmth of his male body, she lay still as fiery fingerlets lit up the blinds in her bedroom. The thunderstorm of last night was over, but the fresh scent of rain hung in the air.

How she would have loved lying in Jordan's arms and watching him sleep—if only she didn't dread his awakening.

She bit her love-swollen lips, her mind flooding with wanton memories. Last night he had loved her as though he'd been insane for her. Blushingly she remembered the last time just before dawn. How his hands had roamed her, and then his lips, his mouth gently caressing the delicate, warm secret of her. He had put his rough cheek against her belly, and then between her thighs again and again. She'd marveled at his doing that, just as she'd marveled at the rapture he seemed to find in giving her the most exquisite, shattering pleasure she'd ever known.

She had learned again that there was beauty in the sensation of touch, a beauty in a man and woman coming to-gether that could bind more deeply than any other kind of beauty, a dark, secret, subconscious beauty that could bind the soul as well.

The thought of giving him up again, of losing him, was unbearable, and yet she had no choice.

The sunlight climbed higher against the blinds, casting golden, scintillating beams across Jordan's dark, exhausted face.

He groaned, and she snuggled closer, wanting to lose herself in his nearness. He opened his eyes, and when he saw her he smiled sleepily, as though it were perfectly natural that he awaken and find himself in bed with her. He closed his eyes again, but his fingertips ran over her taut nipples. She gasped. She heard his breath shorten as his hands explored the hard-tipped mounds that he found so desirable.

She tried to fight the sweet intoxication his caresses aroused.

"Jordan, no."

"Your body keeps saying yes, my love," he whispered teasingly.

That was because awakening and finding him in her bed felt so thrillingly right, even though it was the last thing from right. Unbidden came the tormenting question: was it really unusual for Jordan Jacks to awaken in the arms of a new woman he'd just made love to? Not that she was a new woman. But then, in a way she was.

She caught herself. Why did it matter, when she was determined to have nothing more to do with him? Last night he'd practically forced himself on her. It was she who had left him and divorced him. If he'd had other women through the years, many of them famous and far more beautiful than she, it was what she had wanted, wasn't it?

And yet, she couldn't stop herself from wondering how he felt about her now that he'd had her again. Had last night meant anything to him? Or had he only wanted her all these years because he'd believed she was dead? Had she intrigued him only because she'd walked away? Now that he'd had her, would he really want her?

Stop it! What did any of that matter? After today, she would have nothing more to do with him.

His hands ran down her body, and she discovered suddenly that for all his seeming drowsiness he wanted her again. And fiercely. She caught her breath as he eased himself into her soft, yielding flesh. She moved against him, her passion suddenly as wild as his.

"You're quite something," he murmured, his hands pressing into the small of her back. The warmth of his breath stirred in her hair.

In spite of herself, she laughed huskily.

"So now it's yes, love," he taunted.

She tried to move away from him.

He laughed and pulled her back, closer than before, making love to her, swift, violent love, until she clung to him tightly. Her body felt burned by an inner flame. Every inch of her hot skin was alive with rippling pulsations, and she moaned at the sheer exquisiteness of the pleasure she found in him.

Her bones became fluid. Her entire body melted into a waxen oneness with his. Then suddenly he shuddered, and his eclipse of passion brought hers. They held on to one another, the spasms of his powerful body caressing hers.

She lay locked in his arms, her breasts rubbing against his chest, the timeless rhythm of their bodies subsiding. Then she opened her eyes, the brightness in the sunlit room dazzling her just as his warm, tender smile dazzled her.

Never had a man looked more in love, she thought with sudden fear, and in the afterglow of mutual rapture a new terror began to grow inside her. He was not going to let her go. No matter how she fought him. He would use everything in his power to make her do what he wanted.

And he would win. She knew too well that he was a man who always got what he wanted.

She wondered how long it would take him to learn that she was right, that she would never be the wife that a man of his immense talent and fame needed?

Their inevitable quarrel came two hours later, after breakfast. They were at the kitchen table with Melanie, who was obviously in awe of Jordan. He had been attentive to her all morning, and Melanie was aglow.

Before breakfast father and daughter had gone outside, taking Melanie's guitar, and Jordan had helped her with her music. Through the open kitchen windows, Gini had heard their muffled voices as they talked and laughed between songs.

Melanie was overjoyed by her parents' unexpected reunion, and Gini was furious that Jordan had deliberately not told Melanie that the situation wasn't going to be permanent.

After his second cup of coffee Jordan said, "Why don't I wash and you dry, Melanie?"

He had begun to stack the dishes, when Gini forced herself to say stonily, "That won't be necessary, Jordan. You're our guest. We'll do them after you've gone," deliberately placing emphasis on "after you've gone."

He stared back at her, his dark face suddenly haggard and drawn, yet determined. Guiltily, Gini realized how exhausted he must be, both from his tour and from not getting enough sleep last night.

"I said I'd do them and I intend to, Gini. And as for my leaving, that will only be temporary, I assure you." His voice was tightly controlled. He turned toward his daughter. "Melanie, on second thought, I think it might be better if your mother dries. She and I need to have a talk."

"That was a euphemism if ever I heard one," Gini stormed as soon as Melanie had gone.

Jordan set the stack of dishes down and they were instantly forgotten. "I have no intention of walking out of your life, Gini. Especially not after last night."

"Last night was your idea. Not mine."

"Are you going to try to convince me that you didn't want me to stay last night? That I forced you?"

"In a way you did."

His lips curved into a cynical jeer. She hated the way his knowing eyes stripped away her defenses.

She reddened and lashed out angrily. "No matter what happened between us last night, the last thing I want is to compound that mistake by making it a permanent arrangement."

She whirled and would have run from the kitchen to lock herself in her bedroom until he left, but his arm snaked forward and he gripped her wrist. He yanked her hard against his chest. Gini struggled to break free, but his arms pinned her to his body. He whitened with pain though he said nothing. Remembering he was hurt, she stopped fighting him. His grip loosened, but only fractionally.

"Gini, you're my wife."

"Your ex-wife."

"A mere technicality that can be easily corrected."

"A reality. Thirteen years, to be exact. A lifetime. Or have you forgotten?"

"Damn it," he muttered beneath his breath. "You're coming back to me."

"And do I have anything to say about this? It's only my life. And Melanie's."

"And Melanie's," he echoed ever so softly. Ever so meaningfully.

Gini chewed her bottom lip, her heart filling with guilt. It was impossible for her to meet his eyes. "I don't want to talk about Melanie."

"But I do," Jordan persisted relentlessly. "She and I talked this morning. She wants to come to California."

"Jordan, how could you involve her in this?"

"She is our child. It's her future, too. Your one-woman struggle to keep your head above water financially may be your idea of a blissful challenge, but it's not Melanie's." His eyes ran over the torn linoleum floor, the missing tiles on the drain board, the chipped sink and the stack of unpaid bills by the telephone on the table. "She told me she feels very insecure over money. She's been afraid, too, of having only one parent."

"That's only been since my accident."

"And what will happen if you should have another crisis?" His voice gentled. "Look, don't get me wrong. I think you've done a wonderful job with Melanie. She's bright, well adjusted and sweet. But she needs two parents. Even if I were fool enough to walk out of here without fighting for you, I'd help you financially. Surely you know that. But there's more than money involved. There's love. There's being a family. For thirteen years I've done without those things. There would be advantages for you as well. If you didn't have to work so hard to make a living, you would have more time for her. She needs you, Gini, and whether you like it or not, she needs me."

It was a long time before Gini could reply, and when she did her voice was so low he could barely hear her.

"I guess you know you've backed me into a corner, Jordan. I'm sure Melanie's listening to everything we're saying, and she'll resent me forever if I don't do what you want."

"Gini, I want you back."

"So you keep saying. But I wonder. Once you see how poorly I fit into your glamorous life, will you still feel that way?"

"My glamorous life has been lonely as hell, and from the look of things around here, yours hasn't been a picnic either."

"I can't believe it's possible for us to work things out."

"There's only one way you'll ever know."

A silent sigh of apprehension quivered through her. Her skin felt cold where his hands held her. She wondered how much more she could endure. She was so afraid she wanted him far more than he could ever want her. And if things didn't work out, she would be left bereft, and he would go on, forgetting her as he must have forgotten so many other women. But she owed something to Melanie. They both did.

"All right," she agreed reluctantly at last. "We'll come. For the summer. After that we'll have to see."

"I have two weeks left on my tour. By then school will be out."

"Yes." It all seemed so unreal.

He rocked her in his arms. "More than anything I want you to be happy. Gini."

His sudden gentleness and concern caught her unaware, and her pulse accelerated. She felt alarmed that she was so vulnerable to him, to his casual touch, to any imagined note of kindness in his voice. An odd tightness gripped her throat, and she was slightly breathless. Suddenly she realized how easy it would be to let the powerful attraction she felt for him simply carry her away. But that would be much much too dangerous. It would hardly resolve the multitude of differences between them.

He had told her he wanted her to be happy. Suddenly she had to say something hurtful, because for her own salvation she had to put some emotional distance between them.

"And do you think you can *force* me to be happy, Jordan?"

She felt him tense. "If I have to," he replied in a dangerously quiet voice.

He had not released her. His fingers were lightly stroking her arm, and this caressing motion was much more disturbing than his words. She despised herself for the tingling warmth his hands and his nearness so effortlessly aroused.

"Jordan, there's something I have to know." There was a breathless catch in her voice.

"Yes."

She couldn't avoid his eyes, and she was nearly overcome by the sensation that she could willingly drown in those black pools. "Is there someone else in your life? Another woman?" she asked weakly. Oh, why had she asked that? It would be all too obvious how deeply she cared.

His fingers were in her hair. "There is someone I've been seeing," he confessed. "But that's all over now that I've found you again. I'm going to talk to her immediately. She'll have to understand. Gini, you're the only woman I've ever loved."

The ruthlessly determined note underlying his avowal of love for her, and his intention to quickly rid himself of the other woman, made Gini shiver. When he was tired of her, would he abandon her with the same ease he'd abandoned this other woman?

What would she do if he did? How would she survive?

He sensed her doubt. "Gini, forget everything you've read about me or heard about me. Most of it is media hype. There have been women through the years, and this last was a more meaningful relationship than any of the others. But I never found again what *we* had. Maybe that's why I'm so determined to have you back."

Oh, she wanted to believe him.

He bent his head to hers, determined to convince her in the only way he knew how. She felt the stirring warmth of his breath on the exposed nape of her neck, and the sensuous pressure of his lips exploring that special pleasure place sent a delicious tremor through her.

His hands slid over her, molding her body even more closely against his. Primitive longing flowed in her veins.

"Say you'll try to find your way back to me, Gini. That's all I ask."

His mouth was against her ear, his teeth nibbling the soft, sensitive fleshy tip of her earlobe.

"I can't think when you do that," she said breathing raggedly.

"I don't want you to think. I want you to feel," Jordan commanded.

That was the whole problem. Her feelings for him had always been too intense. She didn't want to promise him anything when she was shaky with desire for him.

She wrenched away from him and stumbled a step back from the temptation of his embrace. Then she stopped, trembling with emotion. His furious black gaze bored into her.

"All right, Gini," Jordan said, his hoarse voice tightly clipped as he strove for control. "Have it your own way! I'll see you in two weeks. But you're coming then, if I have to find some way to force you."

"Why can't you understand it's not as easy for me as it is you?" she murmured wearily. "I can't make promises on such a flimsy basis. Passion is not necessarily love. If we make commitments today before we're sure, we may regret them tomorrow."

"That's where we're different, then, Gini. I don't give a damn about tomorrow."

He moved toward her then and slid his arm around her waist. She thought perhaps he meant to kiss her again, and she wasn't sure she was strong enough to resist giving in to her feelings a second time. One taste of his lips and she would have promised him anything.

But instead of taking her in his arms again, Jordan's hand propelled her forward. "Since everything's settled, I might as well go," he said. "But first, don't you think we should tell Melanie of our happy decision?"

His slashing smile and the soft irony in his lazy drawl mocked the bitter turmoil in both their hearts.

His black gaze swung over her. His face was now a cool, dark blank, and she wondered frantically if what he demanded would ever be possible.

Seven

———

Gini leaned across Melanie, and they both stared out the window as Jordan's Lear jet made its final approach into L.A. International Airport. Samantha meowed frantically and continually from her pet cage on the seat across the aisle.

"Do you think Daddy will at least come to the airport to meet us?" Melanie asked hopefully.

"He said he would try," Gini replied, trying to sound casually indifferent. Jordan's phone calls from California had been decidedly cool ever since he'd stalked out of her house two weeks ago.

He'd said he couldn't fly to Houston himself to pick them up because he'd run into some last-minute problems with an album he was working on and couldn't get away. Of course, Melanie had believed this excuse, but Gini wondered if his reticence to come after them meant he was beginning to have his own doubts about the wisdom of the reconciliation he was forcing. Perhaps breaking up with the woman he was currently seeing had proved more difficult for him than he'd believed.

Gini forced her mind from those disturbing thoughts. If she was going to doubt his word at every turn, she should never have come to California.

"It's all so big," Melanie gasped excitedly, staring at the city.

Gini was glad of the distraction.

Beneath them the awesome metropolis spilled its stacks of chrome and steel buildings from wrinkled brown desert mountains to a blue Pacific.

Within minutes the jet was on the ground, and they were being hurried to a waiting Cadillac limousine by an entourage hired by Jordan. Reporters swarmed on all sides of them, but Jordan's men managed to keep a protective barrier around Gini and Melanie. Samantha kept up a demented yowl from her cage despite Melanie's attempt to comfort her.

Gini's heart stopped beating as she scanned the sea of jostling strangers' faces for Jordan. Three cameras snapped simultaneously in her face, and she tripped over a curb. One of the men beside her took her arm to help her.

"He didn't come!" Melanie cried, her young voice desolate.

"No," Gini echoed, "he didn't come." Why did that fact fill her with such leaden emptiness?

Mother and daughter reached the white Cadillac, and the chauffeur was opening the door. People bustled around them, yelling, pushing, begging them to answer a few questions or to turn and pose for pictures.

From inside the luxurious interior of the car came the soft, cool irony of a woman's voice in greeting.

"Welcome to L.A., Gini," Felicia purred, scooting across a leather seat to make room for them. People began to pound on the windshield. Cameras clicked wildly. Jordan's music pulsated from stereo speakers within the car.

Felicia was smiling as though she found the situation immensely amusing.

Gini climbed gratefully inside. She was beginning to feel unnerved by all the confusion. Samantha's yellow eyes were wild; her gray fur stood on end as Melanie slid her cage onto the seat.

"I do hope they don't break the windshield wipers again," Felicia said mildly, lowering the volume on the stereo. "Not that it rains very often out here."

The scent of lilacs filled the car. Doubtless, Felicia's perfume.

Reclining negligently against white leather, her body a svelte, feline curl, Felicia wore the confident look of a woman who knew she was absolutely stunning in her lavender sweater dress. Her golden hair was bound jauntily in a vivid headband that matched her dress. Her accessories were black-and-gold enamel earrings. Felicia's perfect California tan was as perfect as ever. So were her long lavender nails. Felicia reeked of money, success and Beverly Hills sophistication. She was the kind of woman Gini had always thought Jordan needed at his side.

In her neat blue silk sale dress, Gini felt gauche in comparison, and she folded her hands tensely in her lap to hide her short nails.

Soon the Cadillac was speeding north along the San Diego Freeway toward Malibu. Gini felt increasingly depressed as she viewed the blur of sights and listened to the drone of Felicia's voice telling Melanie what everything was. Though Felicia didn't say it aloud, Gini intuitively deciphered her message. "L.A. is for the rich and talented. It's my kind of town, Gini Jacks. It will never be yours."

Orange trees were startling against the background of snowcapped mountains. Purple jacaranda trees were in full bloom. Medians overflowed with poppies and petunias and a profusion of other riotous blossoms. Palm-lined boulevards and white palaces with red tiled roofs were bathed in beneficent sunshine. All these things only made Gini more aware of how lost and alienated she felt. Everything seemed so different from Texas.

A feeling of dread went through her. Oh, how would she ever get used to all this? Would this ever feel like home? Could she belong? If only Jordan had come to the airport she might not have felt so besieged by all her old doubts.

As if Felicia were a mind reader, her cool voice broke into Gini's uncertain thoughts.

"I hope you can understand that Jordan felt he was much too busy to drive to the airport to pick you up. I told him I would handle the last-minute business details with his album. I usually do. But he insisted on taking care of them himself today. He didn't seem to think you'd mind."

"Of course, I understand," Gini lied miserably, Felicia's words of comfort having upset her all the more.

"I hoped you would," Felicia said sweetly. Her eyes gleamed with some fierce emotion that jarred with the saccharine voice she affected, but Gini was too unhappy to notice.

The driver exited the freeway and headed toward the ocean. Lebanese cedars, palms, and a few olive trees were familiar yet unreal. Bright flowers bloomed everywhere. Gini scarcely noticed these things. She was lost in thought.

Her life had changed so quickly she no longer felt she could take anything for granted. Two weeks ago she'd been a schoolteacher struggling to make ends meet. Life had not been easy, but it had definitely been simpler. More within her grasp. Now she was to live as though she were rich, richer than she'd ever dreamed of being. She'd be living with a man whose fame was legendary. But where would she fit into his life?

"There won't be that much to it," Jordan had said. "The people out there are the same as people anywhere."

Before Jordan left Houston, he'd given her an enormous check. Gini had paid all her bills with the money, but it had brought her little pleasure since she had not earned it herself. Also, the money had merely served to emphasize the great gap that separated them.

When the Cadillac arrived at Jordan's Malibu mansion, Lisa, one of the maids, informed them that Jordan was still at the recording studio. Thus, it was Felicia who, with a thoroughly proprietary air, showed Gini through the house.

"The floors, of course, are all travertine marble," Felicia cooed as she ushered them from one lavish room to another.

Gini wasn't looking at the floors. She was gaping in amazement at the forest someone had planted in the living room. There was even a waterfall nestled beneath the deep shade of a lush tree.

"The outside pool is black marble, of course," Felicia continued.

"Of course," Gini echoed. She had not been able to help that bit of sarcasm. Not that it fazed Felicia.

"My decorator explained at the time that marble was the only way to go. Jordan, you see, left all these decisions to me." While Gini was still pondering the possessively intimate tone Felicia used every time she referred to Jordan, Felicia was clicking off the features she knew by heart: red granite kitchen counters, Hawaiian koa wood flooring, three hundred square feet of glass ceiling.

The views of the Pacific were wonderful, and the grandeur and beauty of the house were breathtaking—if one went for the overdone. There was certainly nothing understated about this house. Gini could not help wondering uneasily if it was a reflection of the man Jordan had become.

Suddenly Gini felt weary and lost in all the magnificence, and Felicia's incessant chatter only served to make Gini feel more ill at ease. She was thankful when a telephone call interrupted the unendurable tour just as Felicia had begun her explanation of the computer that monitored the elaborate security system. After the call, Felicia left abruptly.

Melanie, who was delighted rather than intimidated by the house, skipped up the stairs to unpack and admire her own room. Gini decided to finish looking at the mansion on her own. She struggled not to appear wide-eyed with astonishment before the servants, who seemed perfectly at home amidst this overblown luxury. This was especially difficult because she found the size of the staff even more impressive than the house, marble pool, loggia, tennis courts and inside forest.

Imagine having a house full of people all the time. There were two bodyguards who constantly patrolled the house and grounds, two cooks, two maids, a gardener and a maintenance man, who was working on the pump for the pool.

In the kitchen Gini paused to watch the cooks preparing dinner. They were planning a Mediterranean onion soup for the first course, sautéed chicken breasts in lemon cream, parslied rice pilaf, and an apple pudding for dessert. When she offered to help, they looked embarrassed and muttered something to her in broken English. Gini, realizing she'd made a mistake, reddened and quickly left the kitchen.

What did you do when you were suddenly a millionaire's wife and had nothing to do?

She walked aimlessly outside into the cool darkness of the shaded loggia and admired the brilliant cobalt-blue waters that rolled lazily against a golden beach. After a while this view brought peace to her soul, and she sank down into the plump cushion of a beige sofa, kicked her high heels off, and curled her feet beneath her legs.

Lulled by the salt-scented breezes and the sound of the surf, she fell asleep. The sun grew bright and fat, and someone tiptoed across the polished tiles of the loggia and covered her with a light woolen shawl before he lowered the sun shades so she would not be disturbed by the brilliance of the setting sun.

When Gini did awaken more than an hour later, a red sun hovered upon the horizon. The water was tinted the color of flame. Two gulls swooped and screamed overhead. Several surfers were riding the waves. A jogger in blue warm-ups was running the length of the beach.

Gini heard a familiar shout of glee and recognized Melanie's voice. Beneath on the fiery sand, she saw Melanie loping to catch a Frisbee Jordan had tossed. Jordan laughed as Melanie lunged and caught it in midair and then plummeted into the sand.

Father and daughter were so natural together. It hardly seemed possible that they scarcely knew one another. In that moment Gini was almost glad Jordan had forced her to bring Melanie to California. Melanie had needed a father for so long. Then Gini remembered all her doubts, and her expression grew grave. What if Jordan was only using Melanie to get his way?

Gini arose and walked to the railing where she could have a better view of them. This movement caught Jordan's eye, and he looked up and beheld her hesitantly arrested at the edge of the loggia, her brown curls gilded with the scarlet fire of the setting sun, several loose tendrils blowing against her rosily flushed cheeks.

The Frisbee zinged past him, but he never saw it. He only saw her.

He was so all-male and heart-stoppingly virile she could not stop looking at him either. Cutoffs fitted his narrow hips snugly, molding the shape of his powerful thighs. He wore no shirt. Her vision was drawn to his wide, teak-brown shoulders and firmly muscled chest, to the narrowness of his waist. He was wet, as though he'd recently taken a swim in the surf. His feet were bare. He didn't look like a wealthy rock star, but like a man who was having a wonderful time with his daughter.

She hated the way she instantly felt—as if something were freezing inside her. She was almost sick with longing.

In his eyes, Gini saw some wild emotion before he quickly masked it with the coolness he had shown her ever since he'd left her in Houston. His handsome face was suddenly strained and tense. His black eyes seared her.

She was aware of his gaze moving lower, lingering upon the silk bodice of her dress where the wind shaped the flimsy material against the curve of her breasts.

She stiffened and was about to go inside when his voice arrested her flight. "Gini, don't go in. Come on down and join us," he called up to her. His tone was deliberately cool. "The stairs to the beach are over there." He pointed to her left.

Her heart had begun to thump chaotically. Why couldn't he leave her alone? "I—I'm afraid I'm not yet up to chasing Frisbees."

"Then I'll do the Frisbee chasing," he said, jamming white-knuckled fists deeply into his pockets. It was obvious he didn't like her rejecting him. "You just come down so I can welcome you to California."

Still she hesitated. His fierce, piercing gaze tore from her what little remaining courage she had.

The moment grew long and tense. She was conscious of Melanie watching her. Reluctantly Gini made her way down the steps. It would have hardly seemed civil to deny such a simple request.

She stood before them, the man she loved and their daughter, and never had she felt more at a loss. His black eye had almost disappeared, and she was glad of that.

"I'm sorry I couldn't come to the airport," he said more gently, his coolness seeming to melt. "I don't blame you for being mad."

"I'm not mad."

"Then I don't blame you for whatever you're feeling." He came toward her and took her hand in his warm clasp, and she shivered at the electric contact between them.

He towered over her, his body lean and hard. Try as she would not to stare, she drank in every detail of him as though she'd been starved for him these past two weeks.

And she'd told herself she hadn't wanted to come!

"It's okay. Melanie and I understood why you couldn't come to the airport," she muttered ungraciously, trying to pull her hand from his.

His grip tightened. He was determined to keep her at his side. "No, it's not okay. It was inexcusable." His mouth thinned with anger though the emotion did not seem directed toward her. "And to make it up to you, I want to take you out to dinner tonight."

"But your cooks are putting together the most fabulous meal," Gini protested.

"That was Felicia's idea, not mine," he said grimly. "This is our night, and I won't have her orchestrating it."

"I don't mind staying home, Jordan."

"But I do."

Their eyes met, his warm and devouring, hers nervous and uncertain. Then Gini stared out across the beach, where red waves licked and withdrew, leaving the sand a dark, wet coppery red. Melanie had run off and was poking a stick down a hole, seemingly oblivious to her parents' awkwardness in dealing with one another. Yet Gini knew she was very aware of it, and that she'd left to give them privacy.

"I know all this must seem strange," Jordan began, gesturing to the mansions that lined the beach, "especially when you're not used to it. But maybe if you give it some time—"

"I told you I can't make promises, Jordan."

"Right."

He looked grim again, and she hated that.

Suddenly he said, "I've done my share of wondering if I did the right thing by choosing music for my career. I lost you...and Melanie. I know musicians are considered wild and unstable as a bunch, but, you know, that's a stereotype that doesn't fit me. I'm just a man who communicates his feelings with his music. I must touch people, or they wouldn't like my music. And I've never done anything onstage or offstage I'm ashamed of. A lot of my fans are middle-aged. Even my parents have decided that my career hasn't damaged me."

"You don't have to defend yourself to me, Jordan."

"Why do I feel like I do, then?"

"I guess it's my fault in a way," she admitted.

"If you could only believe in me as a man instead of seeing an image that isn't me at all," he said. A haunting sadness had come into his deep voice. "Sometimes I wish I were a lawyer back in Austin or Pennsylvania. We'd probably have had three or four kids by now."

"And you would have always felt something was missing in your life," she finished with a little half sigh.

"I've felt like that anyway without you."

"Poor little rich boy," she taunted.

He pulled her to him. "Not anymore. I have everything I want now."

His mouth nuzzled the soft brown hair covering her temples.

"Don't," she murmured. "Not out here."

"I'm not ashamed of how I feel about you," he countered roughly. "Why should you be?"

His hand curved along her slender throat, turning her face toward him. She seemed to stop breathing as his eyes explored every inch of her face. His mouth closed over her parted lips. The pressure of his hand at the small of her back aligned her body with his.

Through her thin silk dress she could feel the hard power of his thighs against her body. The wetness of his cutoffs dampened her hips. He let his fingertips stray from her white collar down over the edge of her breast. "Why do you have to be so beautiful," he asked softly, "and so determined to deny something that could make both of us very happy?"

Again his mouth sought hers, and she shivered from its burning intensity. His hands stroked her. She felt the solid beat of his heart, the bronzed hardness of his chest mashed against her breasts.

His lips were hard and passionate. His kiss ignited an inner fire that slowly spread. He tasted pleasantly salty from his swim in the ocean.

Gini ended her passive acceptance of his mouth and began to return his kisses. At her response, his mouth hardened in demanding possession.

At last Jordan withdrew his lips from hers. "For two weeks I've thought only of this moment. Welcome to California, Gini," he whispered huskily against her mouth.

His words brought her up sharply. She remembered where they were, and she fought to push him away even though desire raced like wildfire through her arteries.

"I think we'd better stop," she said breathlessly.

He let her go. "For now," he agreed with a smile. His dark eyes were brilliant. "But later..."

Later there would be no stopping him.

That evening he drove her to the Beverly Hills Hotel, and she tried not to show her awe of the famous landmark, its green-and-pink stucco buildings set on twelve artistically landscaped and lushly planted acres. Hand in hand they walked along meandering paths lined with giant palm trees and leafy foliage, quietly talking. The night was clear and black and star dotted. A waxing moon peeped through the trees. Melanie had insisted on staying in Malibu, and Gini suspected her daughter was hoping they would have a romantic evening together.

Gini and Jordan had drinks in the world famous Polo Lounge. Heads turned when they entered the room. Gini was aware of people whispering discreetly.

"You've made quite a stir your first night out on the town," Jordan teased gently.

"Correction. You're the one making a stir. No one could possibly be interested in me."

"How wrong you are." His hot dark eyes ran over her lingeringly. "I am."

She was wearing a shimmery white cocktail dress with a scooped neckline above which her breasts swelled enticingly.

Beneath his gaze she blushed. "Behave yourself."

"You should have worn something...er...more schoolteachery, then, if you didn't want me to notice you," he replied.

"I'll keep that in mind in the future."

"Please, don't."

Celebrities came up to them, and Jordan introduced her to all of them as his wife. Jordan paid no attention to her embarrassed answers and blushes, and his friends seemed to accept her as well. They even acted as if they found her charming.

When they were alone, Gini shyly chided him.

"Jordan, you are deliberately misrepresenting our relationship."

"No, love," he replied, his voice low and husky. "We were married, and very soon we will be again. You are the only wife I ever intend to have." Beneath the table his hand stole possessively over hers.

Much later they dined in the hotel's restaurant for gourmet fare, the Coterie, which was done charmingly in peach and coral, with gold-and-copper accents and lacquered, burnished sienna woodwork.

When a famous movie star invited them to join him for dinner, Jordan politely refused.

"I hope you don't mind my turning Michael down," he whispered conspiratorially after the star had gone. "But I want to be alone with you."

Was that the reason, or was she afraid that she would not fit in among such glamorous people?

Jordan was attentive, and the food was so marvelous and so splendidly served that she soon forgot her doubts. Hors d'oeuvres were crepes Bombay with curry. Her entree, a poached trout stuffed with salmon mousse in wine sauce, was served so beautifully that she laughingly told Jordan it seemed a crime to eat such a culinary masterpiece. He chuckled and assured her it would be more of a crime to let it go to waste.

"What's worse than old fish?" he joked.

"You do have a point," she agreed, lifting her fork decisively.

Jordan entertained her with legends about the hotel. "There's a certain Texas oil millionaire who always expects to be served bear steaks from Alaska when he's in town."

Gini laughed. "Perhaps I should develop a fancy for Texas armadillo steaks so there'll be a story about me."

"I don't want there to be stories about you. I want you all for myself." He reached across the table and caressed her hand.

For dessert Gini and Jordan shared a sumptuous chocolate soufflé Grand Marnier for two.

After that he took her on a drive along the ocean, his powerful Maserati roaring along the curving road at a speed that made her blood tingle with excitement, yet that seemed, in that marvelous car, on this most magic of nights, to be no speed at all.

Soon they had left the diamond lights of the city behind them. Black headlands tumbled into a boiling surf. The wind was in her hair. Gini threw her head back against the leather upholstery and stared at the night-dark sky sprinkled with stars and a moon. She inhaled the balmy air.

She felt terribly young. Or was it only giddiness from the wine she'd drunk that gave her this breathless sensation of expectancy and made her feel she was floating in a dream, as if all the years in between had never been?

Jordan pulled off the road onto a promontory that jutted over the ocean. He braked the car and pulled her into his arms. The Pacific crashed in breakers onto the sand.

"All night I've wanted to do this," he murmured.

A quiver went through her. All night she had wanted him to.

His mouth came down on hers in a sudden rush of hard warmth and passion.

At last they drew breathlessly apart, her heart torn by the painful clash of her feelings.

"Oh, Jordan, I would give anything to be the right woman for you," she admitted weakly.

"You are."

"I should be more glamorous."

"Do you have any idea how I hate it when you say that?" His tone had roughened, and he caught her more tightly against his body. "You keep erecting this barrier between us. Don't ever change, Gini. Don't lose your freshness, your innocence. You are very special in your own way. Too many people out here wear glamour like armor. They're afraid to be themselves."

"So am I."

"You don't have to be. Do I seem all that different from the man you were married to in Austin?"

"You mean if I ignore your fame, fortune, Maserati, and little old Malibu beach palace?"

"You know what I mean, Gini."

She shook her head, feeling a little amazed as she realized that it was true. Fame and wealth had come to him, but he hadn't lost himself.

"You're special," she said quietly.

"So are you."

She could never accept that.

"I'm the same man I was back then, and I still want the same woman. Why is that so hard to believe?"

"It just is."

"Try, Gini, please."

She looked out upon the magnificent black ocean glistening in the moonlight. It would be unfair if she promised something she was far from feeling. No matter how she wanted to please him, she wouldn't let him bully her into that. He had grown beyond her, far, far beyond her.

He let her go, and she sensed his frustration as he silently started the car. Though he drove fast, it seemed forever before they reached his Malibu home. He parked the Maserati in his four-car garage in between the white stretch limousine and a Jeep.

"Why the Jeep, Jordan?" she couldn't resist asking as he helped her out of the car. "It looks sort of out of place."

"You can't be true-blue Malibu unless you have a Jeep," he replied cynically.

Once inside he led her through the living room. She stopped him, determined to ease his tension. Or was she only trying to put off being in their bedroom together alone?

"Really, Jordan, isn't this room a little bit much, even for a star like you? I feel like I'm lost in a jungle."

Jordan's intent gaze swung over the striking room. He felt he was seeing it for the first time in years. There did seem to be an overabundance of tall trees, shrubbery and flowers. The sunken marble fireplace area with its circular couch, all under the immense glass ceiling, probably did strike her as ostentatious.

"Felicia was into trees when she did the room," he said dryly. "She said they would help us breathe."

"That sounds like pure California."

"If you don't like the house, you can change it any way you want."

"I—I wouldn't dream of changing anything. I don't know the first thing about decorating."

He took her in his arms. "Then hire somebody who can translate your ideas into design. You know as much as I do, or anybody else. If changing the house would give you pleasure, do it."

"I could never spend all that money."

"Why not, if I don't care?"

"It would be such a waste."

"Not if you could turn this bizarre palace into a real home."

Gini was surprised by the gentle, almost tender expression that crossed his masculine features. She didn't know how to answer.

Pulling away from him, she said, "I won't change a thing."

"Oh, but you're wrong. You've already changed everything."

"I meant the house," she protested.

"And *I* meant my life."

His chuckle was soft, almost silent, a disarming sound. He drew her against his body and lifted her into his arms.

"What are you doing?"

"Surely it's obvious. The man of the house intends to ravish the lady of the house."

"What if the lady says no?"

"She won't."

"How do you know?"

"I know the lady."

He carried her the rest of the way in silence, letting her down only when they were alone in the luxurious master suite with its panoramic view of the Pacific and its free-standing fireplace. Gini stared at the built-in bed against one wall, and the mirrored doors on the other that opened into a huge mirrored dressing area. She knew that behind those doors the luxury went on and on. There was a sauna, a private sun deck, a four-person whirlpool, a weight room and a music room with a nine-foot concert grand where Jordan worked when he was home.

Jordan went to the stereo and put a record on the turntable. The soft tinkle of sensuous piano music filled the room.

Across the bedroom, their gazes met. His black eyes were intense.

"Debussy," she murmured.

"Your favorite composer."

He was struggling out of his jacket and slinging it onto a suede chair. She tried to ignore the implied intimacy of the room, of what he was doing.

"You remembered," she managed in a barely audible voice. She was inordinately pleased, but she was determined not to let him know how pleased she was.

His tie had joined his discarded jacket, and he was stripping out of his shirt. "I remember everything about you, darling. When you packed your bag and walked out of my life, you took my soul." Something savage had come into voice. He threw his shirt onto the floor and strode across the room toward her.

"You seem to have done pretty well without it."

"What could you know about how I've done? You're determined to blind yourself to the truth. All you want to see is my fame and wealth. You see this house, but you don't see me. I'm a man, Gini. I need you."

"Do you, Jordan? How? Just for sex?"

Her questions infuriated him. Black fires blazed in his eyes. His face went white as he fought a losing battle to control his temper. Then he yanked her against his body in one fluid movement. His arms circled her, crushing her against his length.

"You always go for the jugular, don't you?" he ground out. "Yes. I want you for sex. Is that a crime? I've done without you for thirteen years."

"Maybe without *me*, but not without."

Pain and jealousy had driven her to say that—jealousy over all the beautiful women she imagined he'd had through the years. Her own insecurity and his awesome fame stood in the way of her believing him.

His fingers slipped to her shoulders, tightening convulsively as if he wanted to shake the truth into her. Then he regained control.

"No, not without," he admitted wearily. "I'm not going to lie to you about that, Gini. I've never lied to you. But no other woman has ever had that unique quality you have. There's something between us that's magic. There always has been. I know you feel it, too."

Gini stared into the chiseled, leather-tanned features, into those compelling dark eyes, and she forgot about his fame and money. This was Jordan the man, her husband, and he seemed to need her as much as she needed him.

She swayed against him. His hands moved over her, cupping her breasts, moving lower to her waist, to her hips, the intimate explorations of his hands sizzling through her like electric shock waves. Then he caught her to him so tightly she couldn't breathe, and his mouth covered hers in a long, punishing kiss she had no strength to resist.

He drank from her mouth, demanding nothing less from her than total surrender. He was determined to dominate her, to make her feel the dangerous, pulsating sensuality that held him in thrall, to enslave her as he was enslaved.

She responded to the fire of his kiss in every fiber in her being. She felt she was without life, without breath except for what he gave her with his hard, furious kisses. Desire swept through her in heavy, drugging waves.

A crescendo of piano notes grew wildly as he lifted her into his arms and carried her to the bed. He touched a button somewhere and the room melted into velvet darkness. There was only the moonlight outside glistening upon the crashing waves, the spew of white foam dashed against black rocks, the all-enveloping romantic music, the velvet sensuality of heated skin touching heated skin.

He found the zipper at the back of her gown, and within seconds he slid the gauzy fabric over her voluptuous curves and tossed it onto the carpet. Her filmy lingerie followed quickly afterward until her pale body gleamed in the soft light. He stood up and undressed, and her luminous eyes followed his every movement, reveling in the glorious male beauty of him as she witnessed the undeniable evidence of his desire for her. His dark eyes burned down into her face.

Slowly he lowered his hot naked body to cover hers once more. She felt the scorching heat of him to the marrow of her bones. His mouth came down on hers in a long, hard kiss. Then he kissed each eye, each winged brow, her cheeks and her throat.

He embraced her closely, trembling, burying his face in her hair. His voice was low and husky. "I love you, my darling Gini. I love you. What will I have to do to convince you?" There was a shudder of suppressed agony in the question.

Her back arched; a small moan of pleasure escaped her as his warm, seeking lips moved over her breasts to her belly and then lower to taste the feminine essence of her.

She felt his bristly cheek against the soft inside of her thigh, his mouth caressing her with an ever deepening intimacy and heat.

Her blood surged, her heartbeat sounding in her ears. His moist kisses left her reeling in a dizzying whirlpool of feelings.

"Oh, Jordan, I want you. Make love to me," she pleaded.

He chuckled triumphantly and brought his lips to her mouth again. His tongue went into her mouth, probing, tantalizing. She responded, shivering, eager, caressing his shoulders with her hands, moving her body beneath his until he was so aroused he felt she was driving him to madness.

Still he waited, wanting to savor the deliciousness of her. Her trembling response, her supple body, everything about her enflamed him. The scent of her, sweet as flowers, cool with her innocence yet spiced by the aphrodisiac fragrance of her womanliness, sharpened his desire for her.

His blood raced.

"Love me, Jordan."

His hands moved on her gently, making them both shudder as he adjusted her body beneath his.

That night was like no other in his life. She was his in the way he had dreamed of and longed for. She was wanton, wild, abandoned. She made love to him with her lips and her tongue, her mouth exploring every part of his body.

He took her time after time, wanting to know again and again her need of him, reassuring himself that at last she was really his.

She loved him that night hopelessly, blindly, as again and again he wakened her body to searing heights of pleasure. Afterward, when she lay cradled in his arms, she would have told him how she loved him had he asked. But he did not. Drowsily, just before she fell asleep in his arms, she promised herself she would tell him in the morning.

But in the morning he was gone.

Eight

When Gini awoke that morning, brilliant sunlight was flooding Jordan's vast bedroom. She sat up groggily. The ocean was bright shimmering silver.

Then she rolled over on the beige silk sheets and reached languidly for Jordan, longing to curl into his hard warmth, only to find him gone, his rumpled pillow the only evidence that he had lain beside her. Across the room the clothes he had carelessly discarded on the suede chair were gone as well.

Wanton memories flooded her mind, and even though she was alone, her cheeks colored hotly. Had that abandoned creature who had loved him so shamelessly really been her? She remembered the power of his arms circling her, the heat of his kisses, the passionate need he had had of her.

What was there between them that could evoke such excesses of emotion? Yet she had reveled in the mad splendor between them. Even now she felt no guilt. She felt gloriously contented and completely satisfied. Perhaps there really was something special between them even for him, something he could never find with another woman.

She blushed again, then, smiling to herself, she arose, feeling strangely giddy, expectant, yet excitedly pleased at the thought of going down and finding Jordan. How she longed to share the day with him, to share everything with him. The emptiness of the past years were gone. Instead she faced a world full of dazzling promise.

She went into the bathroom and sprinkled scented bubble powder into a marble tub that was large enough for four people. Then she ran hot water into the tub.

As she bathed she leisurely went over the events of last night, the elegant Polo Lounge, Jordan's attentiveness during the most fabulous meal of her life, their drive along the moonlit coast in his wonderful car and then the shameless rapture she'd known in his arms.

She relived every moment, each touch, each look, every sound. Oh, how he had cried out when she began to explore him with her mouth. She sank lower in her bubbled bathwater and giggled in sheer delight as she remembered Jordan's harsh, ragged groans, the way he'd cried her name as her lips and tongue traveled in a hot path from his knee up the inside of his thigh.

When she was dressed, Gini raced as quickly as she could downstairs to find him. Jordan was not in the living room, though Sam was curled defiantly on a suede couch, looking very much at home amidst her luxurious surroundings. Nor was Jordan outside on the loggia. The beach was deserted. Obviously too early for the Malibu crowd.

She heard the clink of china from the dining room and pushed the door open, her heart thudding in excitement. "Jordan?" There was a breathless note in her voice.

"He's already gone, my dear," came that cool, sophisticated tone Gini dreaded more than any other.

Gini tried to conceal her bitter disappointment as her eyes met Felicia's bright, hard gaze. Felicia was as flawlessly lovely as ever, with her blond mane cascading over the shoulders of a dreamily gorgeous milk-white silk suit. Her long nails were a lush pink this morning. Gini, who was immediately self-conscious about her simple black slacks and cotton shirt, had no idea that her look of love-tousled radiance annoyed Felicia immensely.

"Good morning, Gini," Felicia murmured with soft irony. "Coffee, my dear? It's very good. I had Chole make it just the way Jordan and I like it."

Gini just stared at her golden adversary, this woman who seemed so at home playing hostess in Jordan's house, so much more at home in his life than Gini felt at the moment. As always when around Felicia and her aura of designer elegance, Gini felt awkward, only this was worse than usual, because last night's lovemaking had made her more vulnerable.

Where was Jordan? Why had he gone out without even telling her goodbye, as though last night had been nothing out of the ordinary for him? And why did Felicia feel so comfortable in Jordan's house?

Gini collapsed into a chair near Felicia and watched numbly as Felicia filled a cup with steaming coffee and handed it to her.

"I suppose it's time you and I talked," Felicia stated in a velvety voice that held menacing purpose.

"What could we possibly have to talk about?"

"Jordan."

"I really don't think that's wise," Gini whispered falteringly.

"But I do," Felicia replied, her manner that of someone who had long ago grown accustomed to doing exactly as she pleased. "You see, Gini, we both care about him, each in our own way."

Everything was beginning to make an awful kind of sense. Felicia must be the meaningful relationship Jordan had spoken to Gini about in Houston.

Gini stared at Felicia in amazement. This startling discovery was s shock, and yet in some unfathomable way she'd suspected. It was just that Gini had expected someone softer, younger, someone less awesomely competent than Felicia.

Though Gini knew almost nothing about the specifics of Jordan's career, she knew that Felicia was his business manager, and he would never have kept her all these years if she weren't a good one. There was undoubtedly some sort of contract between them. Felicia's constant presence in their lives would have to be endured.

There had never been any hint of a romantic attachment between Felicia and Jordan in the newspapers, and that could only mean that Jordan had cared for Felicia much more than he had cared for any other woman.

"He was dating you, then, before his concert in Houston?" Gini asked weakly. Why was it so important to have this confirmed by Felicia?

"Yes. We had an exclusive relationship for over a year until...two weeks ago in Houston."

"I see."

"You may think I'm sorry that he found you," Felicia said in carefully measured tones, "and I was at first. But that was before I saw you again and realized how wrong you are in every way for Jordan. For thirteen years he's been in love with a fantasy. He would have married me a long time ago, except your ghost was always there between us. Have you any idea how hard it is to live with a ghost? How hard it is to fight a ghost? I'd rather contend with a real woman any day."

Gini sipped her coffee, and the overlarge draft scalded her mouth and throat all the way down. Quickly she gulped from a glass of water.

Felicia's long-lashed eyes flickered without a trace of sympathy. "You see, Gini, though you haven't changed, Jordan has. He's not the man you knew in Austin. He's a star now, and no matter what he says to the contrary, that puts unusual demands upon him. His needs have become extremely unique and complex. It takes a special woman to give a man like Jordan what he really needs."

"What makes you so sure I'm not that woman?"

"Oh, I know he thinks he wants you right now. He told me everything was over between us, that he has always loved you. I tried to reason with him, and then I realized that I'd rather have you here where Jordan has to deal with you on a day-to-day basis. I doubt it will be too long before he realizes that even he can't resurrect a marriage that has been dead thirteen years...despite the novelty of Melanie. What can you do for Jordan compared to what I can do for him? You'll only hold him back."

Stunned by her words, Gini suddenly realized that Felicia had stopped talking and was eyeing her with cool disdain. She seemed to be awaiting some reply. But what did one say to a woman who was so boldly confident she could win your man that she even dared to tell you so in person?

Feeling trapped, Gini let her gaze dart madly around the luxurious room. Everything Felicia said made sense. The euphoria from last night was gone. In its place were all the doubts she'd tried so hard to fight, and a grief more profound than any she'd ever known.

"I love him," Gini said weakly, feeling the inadequacy of such a simple statement.

"But what good will such love do him?" Felicia asked, still in that same cool voice. "Are you even sure that's love, or just some selfish clinging instinct?"

"I'm sure," Gini replied unsteadily.

"It's ironic, but the only reason he wants you is your ordinariness. You see, all great stars are insecure. Even Jordan. They want to be loved for themselves instead of because of their stardom. You knew him and accepted him when he was a nobody. That's the edge you've had over all other women since. But it won't be enough to keep him. He's grown beyond you. You know it. I know it. The world knows it. And quite soon, Jordan will know it. I'll be here waiting when he wakes up." Felicia stood up and picked up her bag.

"I'm sure you will be." Gini stood up as well, hot color staining her face. It took all her strength not to move until Felicia was completely gone from the house.

Gini was on her way to find Melanie when the telephone rang. It was Jordan.

"Good morning," came the husky resonance of his low drawl. He was using his bedroom voice, and it made her remember last night and the way he'd held her and spoken so softly to her in the silvery moonlight. A wave of involuntary excitement rippled through her, quickly followed by a sensation of poignant sadness because of everything Felicia had said.

"Where are you?" she asked hesitantly.

"At the studio. I'm going over a few last details on that album. Felicia and I got our wires crossed, and she ar-

ranged for me to tape an interview for a talk show to pro-
mote my new video, something I thought she understood
I didn't want to do. But it can hardly be avoided now that
she's committed me. Do you think you can find some way
to amuse yourself until I can get home late this
afternoon?"

"Of course," Gini replied mechanically, though she felt
at a loss.

"Why don't you go shopping?"

A few minutes later she hung up. He'd made no refer-
ence to the romantic evening they had shared, and the
hours until his return loomed before her like a great stretch
of emptiness. She picked up the phone again and dialed the
Houston realtor who was handling the rental of her house.

The young woman's voice was wildly enthusiastic.
"Mrs. King, you'll never guess. I've found a buyer for
your property."

"But I don't want to sell. I thought I made it clear that
I only wanted to lease the house for the summer."

"You're sure? Your husband called the other day and
said I should definitely tell you if we found a prospective
buyer."

"My husband?"

"Yes. The real estate market here is very tight. If
you should change your mind about coming back in the
fall—"

"I don't think I'll be changing my mind no matter what
my . . . husband led you to expect."

Gini replaced the telephone. Her unsigned contract for
the next school year was in her purse. She pulled it out and
signed it and then carefully replaced it in its stamped en-
velope. She would mail it while she was out. Then she went
to find Melanie.

First she and Melanie took the Jeep and drove into Beverly Hills to go shopping. The luxurious stores on Rodeo Drive and Wilshire Boulevard were impressive, but she wandered aimlessly through them without being tempted by any of the expensive items for sale. Though Gini now had the money to buy anything, she was just as intimidated by a pair of shoes for three hundred dollars as she was by a lynx coat for a hundred thousand. She sifted through a stack of hundred-dollar ties and then remembered Jordan hated ties. Besides, he had closets and drawers full of clothes, and she was no longer sure of his tastes. There was no point in shopping for his perfectly appointed house, either, because Felicia had already done that. No use shopping for herself because she would have looked like a child playing dress-up in these glamorous clothes.

Every exquisite boutique only increased her feeling of being in a world where she could never belong. She thought the salespeople eyed her suspiciously, as if they, too, considered her some sort of alien.

Gini and Melanie were heading down La Cienega Boulevard when Gini turned to her daughter and asked, "Why don't we go see what Disneyland's all about?"

Melanie instantly agreed, and as they headed onto the San Diego Freeway toward Anaheim, neither of them noticed the brown Pontiac that had been following them ever since they left Wilshire Boulevard.

Half an hour later Gini pulled into a parking lot at Disneyland. As soon as she and Melanie got out of the Jeep, two men who had parked right behind them ran up and began taking pictures. The younger man, a California golden boy who reminded Gini too forcibly of Felicia for her to like him, bombarded her with personal questions.

"Is it true you're living with Jordan Jacks? And that the two of you have an illegitimate daughter?"

"That's a lie!" Gini hissed, and then she remembered that Felicia and Jordan had both warned her to say nothing to reporters. Gini grabbed Melanie's hand and pulled her toward the gates of the amusement park where a policeman was standing.

"Isn't it true that you threatened Mr. Jacks with a paternity suit if he didn't let you move in?"

"Will you be suing him for palimony?"

Gini's blood began to boil. How could they accuse her of something so vile? Though she tried to ignore the two men, their questions kept coming hard and fast until she was so furious she whirled and launched an attack of her own. She was so angry she hardly knew what she was saying.

"For your information, I'm Jordan Jacks's ex-wife. I divorced him thirteen years ago because I wanted to live my own life, my own way, and I didn't move in with him because I want anything from him now. The only reason I came to California is because Jordan forced me to." Oh dear, that sounded terrible, and it wasn't what she'd meant to say. The men were scribbling rapidly. For the first time she noticed their tape recorder and video camera. "I need to explain," she cried. "That wasn't what I meant."

The men cut her off. "But it was what you said, hon. We've got everything we need, little lady."

They were racing each other back to their car as she called after them.

For Gini the day at Disneyland passed in a blur of misery. She and Melanie visited the different lands, the ice-cream parlors, arcades, and silent films of the world famous amusement park, but none of the events touched

Gini. She was too upset at herself for having lost control with those reporters. They wouldn't even have to twist her words to come up with something vicious to say about Jordan.

Melanie, on the other hand, enjoyed the carefree atmosphere of Disneyland. When Gini expressed her concern over what she had said, Melanie laughed it off. "Daddy will understand. Those guys were so awful, anyone would have gotten mad."

When Melanie and Gini returned to Malibu late that afternoon, things were even worse than Gini had imagined. The big-screen television was blaring in the living room. Felicia and Jordan were standing in front of it in grim silence. Jordan was holding the entertainment section of a newspaper. Even from across the room Gini could read the headline that was splashed boldly across it. "Jordan Jacks kidnaps ex-wife and forces her to live with him."

Gini saw herself on the television screen, her head tipped back in defiant fury, her hands clenched at her sides as she railed at the reporters. "The only reason I came to California is because Jordan forced me to."

Felicia went to the set and switched it off. "I think you've seen enough to understand what I meant."

"Jordan," Gini began. "I—I . . ." She was trembling with the fierce desire to explain, to make things right between them once again.

Jordan looked up and saw her for the first time. For a numbed moment she could only stare at him. She longed to run to him and beg his forgiveness, but she held herself in check, something in his forbidding manner stopping her.

She noted the deep cynical lines carved on either side of his hard mouth. Had she made him terribly unhappy? She couldn't tell, but she hoped suddenly that she hadn't.

He folded the paper and threw it onto the couch. Then he moved toward her, his face a mahogany mask that concealed his thoughts.

"Seems like you two had quite a day," he said in a harsh but controlled tone.

His arms circled Gini. Something brushed the tapering shortness of her brown hair where it curled against her temple, and she realized it was his lips. But his kiss had been cool and distant.

"Daddy, we went to Disneyland, and some awful men pestered Mom. She got real mad at them."

"So I see." He smiled at his daughter as he had not smiled at Gini.

"I think I'll go see what's happening on the beach," Melanie said, sensing that this was what her father wanted.

Jordan nodded his approval, and the three adults watched Melanie's departure in ominous silence.

"Jordan, Gini couldn't have done more damage to your image if she'd deliberately set out to," Felicia said.

"I'm so sorry, Jordan," Gini managed. "I never meant—"

His low voice cut across her sentence. "What's done is done. Don't worry about it. It'll blow over. The press is a challenge for anybody, and everybody makes mistakes."

"Jordan," Felicia interrupted. "I can't understand how you can be so casual about this."

"Because I have you, dear Felicia." There was a hint of cynicism in the twist of his handsome mouth. "I'm sure you'll think of some way to turn this to our advantage."

"Perhaps you could be persuaded to do a personal interview, just this once, Jordan. We could run photographs of you and Gini and Melanie. Gini could tell her side to the press."

"No!" Gini cried. Just why she was so against this idea, she wasn't sure. Perhaps because it was Felicia's. Perhaps it was because she didn't want to commit herself publicly to Jordan. More likely it was simply because she was a very private person and didn't want her life to become common gossip. "I am going to take the advice you originally gave me, Felicia. I never intend to talk to the press again no matter how mad they make me."

"Not even to help Jordan?" Felicia asked with false sweetness.

"I wouldn't be helping Jordan if I did that," Gini replied.

Gini was terribly aware of Jordan's slashing gaze that cut her to ribbons.

She licked her lips and swallowed nervously. His anger was close to the surface, transmitting its charged vibration to her overly sensitive nerve ends. She felt defensive even though she knew he had every right to be angry.

She was never to know what he would have said or done, because an urgent business call from London came for him, and he went to his study to take it.

"I told you you were not the right sort of woman to be married to a star," Felicia said softly.

"I learned a long time ago not to believe everything my enemies tell me, Felicia," Gini replied, marveling at her newfound ability to be so forthright. "Tell Jordan I've gone down to the beach to look for Melanie, if you're still here when he gets off the phone."

"Oh, I'll be here."

"I never doubted it for a minute."

The beach was a replay of the evening before: a sinking sun-tinged cloud, a crimson sky and sand a golden pink. Melanie was nowhere in sight.

Gini decided to take a walk and look for her. She had gone scarcely a hundred yards when a man waved casually from the balcony of the house next to Jordan's. He leaned over the railing, smiling, and Gini was drawn by his friendliness. Perhaps she should go over and introduce herself. Wouldn't she always feel alone if she didn't at least try to make friends?

Slowly she walked up to his house and climbed the wooden stairs that led from the beach to his balcony. She didn't notice that his friendliness had become guarded, that his narrow, tanned face held shock. She didn't know she had broken one of the unspoken rules of Malibu—she had come over to his house uninvited. He had only waved.

He stared at her uneasily, as though he wondered what she wanted from him.

"Hello," she said, thrusting her hand toward his. "I'm Gini Jacks, your next-door neighbor."

His look of shock and displeasure slowly vanished as he gazed into the honesty of her soft golden brown eyes. He smiled charmingly again. "I'm James Storme." His warm hand closed over hers and didn't release it.

"That sounds familiar."

"It should," he returned dryly. He let her go.

She looked at him sharply. He was tall and thin with a shock of unruly blond hair. He wore horn-rimmed glasses. With his thin dark face, he was ugly and yet terribly attractive somehow in a very masculine way. Still, she was almost sure she'd never seen him in a film.

"You're not a movie star, are you?"

He threw back his head and laughed. "Good Lord, no!"

"Don't tell me I've blundered again," she said. "You're probably terribly famous."

"Oh, I am." Laughter lingered in his roughly edged voice.

"I can tell." He took her hand in his again and led her to a chair.

"I keep making all these terrible mistakes," she said.

"I saw you on television a minute ago," he said, understanding in his deep voice.

"I could have died."

"Don't worry about it. A little truth is refreshing sometimes."

"That wasn't what I meant to say."

"It never is. Reporters always slant things their way, even the truth."

Gini and James began to talk with an instant rapport that amazed them both. There was an easiness between them that is sometimes lacking even in lifelong friendships. Gini poured her heart out, and he listened.

"So you're the Gini from Jordan's hit song?"

"Yes."

"Now I know why Jordan's never found anyone out here."

"I'm a little ordinary for the show-biz world."

"That wouldn't have been my choice of words," he said. "You're quite lovely. You have your own style."

His compliment pleased her. "From what I read there were a lot of women in Jordan's life through the years."

"A few more encounters with the press like the one you had today, and maybe you'll learn you can't believe anything you read about people in the papers. I've known Jordan pretty well for a long time, and he's kept to himself mostly. His music has been his mistress."

"I keep wondering if I can ever fit in out here." Again she wondered why she was talking to this man, but for some reason she felt comfortable with him. There was warmth in his eyes, an easiness in his manner. She did not know he was finding the experience as unusual as she was.

"Maybe you should stop worrying about fitting in," he said. "Just do what you want to do."

"I was a teacher in Houston, but if I stay with Jordan..."

"If?"

"I've only promised him the summer. If I stay, I can't teach because I don't want to tie myself down. I wouldn't be able to travel with Jordan, you see. Yet teaching is all I know. I feel at loose ends without it. I don't know what to do with myself. Jordan is wealthy enough so that I don't have to work, yet I need something."

"Maybe you should look on this experience as a unique opportunity. You can now be or do anything you want to."

"But what?"

"That's for you to decide. Oh, dear. Looks like Jordan is none too pleased to discover you up here with me. This may surprise you, Gini, but in the ten years I've known him, I never knew he had it in him to be jealous."

James chuckled as Jordan took the stairs three at time and joined them on the balcony.

"So there you are, Gini," Jordan said accusingly. He forced a smile. "Hello, Storme."

"Nice night," James returned pleasantly.

"You two certainly seem to be enjoying it," Jordan replied.

"Oh, we were," James countered.

At that, Jordan didn't bother to conceal his scowl. "Gini, I've been looking everywhere for you. My parents have come over and they want to see you."

"I told Felicia to tell you where I was," Gini said, waving a quick goodbye toward James as Jordan pulled her toward the stairs.

"Your message didn't mention a heart-to-heart sunset chat on James Storme's balcony," Jordan growled.

They had reached the sand and were walking toward Jordan's mansion. "Jealous?" she asked, keeping her voice deliberately light.

He stopped in midstride and yanked her into his arms. "Damn you. You never used to play games. Did you go to Storme just to make me jealous?"

"Of course not," she answered on a bewildered note, realizing she should never have teased him. "He was just friendly...."

"Just friendly! Storme? He's the most notorious womanizer in L.A. Don't tell me you don't know that."

"I didn't know anything about him until tonight."

"He happens to be one of the most famous directors in the world. Every starlet in this city would sell her soul to share his bed."

"He didn't seem too disappointed I wasn't a starlet hawking my soul."

"Obviously his next-door neighbor's wife will do in a pinch."

"Jordan! He was very nice."

"I'll just bet he was. How do you think I feel? One minute you're telling the world I'm forcing myself on you. The next I find you with James Storme."

In the fiery light of the setting sun, Jordan's features resembled a carved teakwood mask of some fierce pagan war god, harsh and dangerous, ruthlessly compelling.

"Jordan, you have no reason to be jealous. And I'm awfully sorry about what I said to those reporters."

"Do you think I give a damn what you say? All I care about is how you feel."

"You know that what I said isn't how I feel," she said weakly.

In towering silence he regarded her for a long moment. "Do I?" he muttered thickly.

Shyly she reached up on tiptoes and kissed him. At the first tantalizing touch of her mouth grazing his, his arms tightened around her waist. She felt boneless as he tipped her head back and drank deep kisses from her lips. An all-encompassing weakness went through her limbs, dizzying her. Wild drums pounded in her ears. Her fingers curled into his shoulders for support.

"Have I told you I like your hair short like this? I never used to think I would, you know." His hushed voice was a husky caress running the length of her spinal column as he smoothed the glossy curls away from her face.

"We'd better go inside," he groaned, "before I lose all interest in showing you off to my family."

"Yes," she murmured, leaning closer and breathing in the dizzying smell of him.

Later, after his parents had gone and they were in bed, they were able to speak privately again. They lay beside each other, their naked bodies not touching. Jordan's arms were a bronzed crisscross of muscle behind his head.

"Mother and Dad were thrilled about you and Melanie," he said.

Gini's sideways glance sought his carved profile in the dim light, and her heart filled with unwelcome love for him. "Yes," she replied softly, guiltily. Tonight, in discovering his parents' instant warmth and acceptance of Melanie and herself, Gini had finally realized the enormity of what she had done by keeping Melanie's birth a secret and letting Jordan believe she was dead. For thirteen years she had denied four people a treasure that was priceless.

"Nothing has ever made them happier," Jordan continued.

"But how can they forgive me for what I did?" Gini asked at last in a tightly throbbing pain-filled voice.

"They forgave you the minute they saw you," he said gently. "Just as I did. No one could better understand your reservations about my career than they. You know something? Tonight, for the first time since you left me, I felt like I was part of a real family."

She stared miserably into the darkness, saying nothing. Could they ever really be a family? Was Jordan right? Or was Felicia right in her belief that she, Gini, could never be the right wife for him? Gini wasn't sure about anything anymore.

A guitar-string-callused finger tilted her chin toward Jordan's face, forcing her to look into his eyes, and her heart skipped a beat at the warmth in his craggy male face. "Oh, Gini," he murmured. "You've given me so much by coming back to me."

Had she? She remembered his anger over the publicity. She'd publicly humiliated him. What would she do next?

He drew her body closer so that she was snuggling against him. His other hand was stroking her upper arm with pleasant, soothing caresses. Their bodies became intimately entwined. "Promise me you won't take it all away again by leaving me." Gently he brushed his lips against her hair, then against her closed eyelids.

It became difficult for her to breathe because of the erotic stimulation of his caresses. The heated length of his body pressed against hers. They lay still, each savoring the warmth and feel and scent of the other.

Her pulse was rocketing out of control. Before she could answer him, his mouth covered her parted lips, and he kissed her with such shattering mastery that neither of them realized she hadn't promised him what he wanted. They simply surrendered to the sensual needs that were too compelling to be ignored.

Jordan forgot that Gini had promised him nothing, but afterward, as Gini lay awake in the darkness beside the sleeping Jordan, she remembered. As she thought back over all the mistakes she kept making and remembered what Felicia had told her, she knew she wasn't ready to make any promises.

She was more uncertain than ever.

Nine

Two weeks passed. Fourteen nights of sensual rapture in the silvery darkness of Jordan's bedroom with the velvet sound of piano arpeggios rippling softly in the background. Fourteen days of foolish blunders on Gini's part, at least when she interpreted them from Felicia's viewpoint. Why was it that practically everything Gini did was wrong?

Gini began to rise earlier in the mornings so that she could cook Jordan's breakfast herself and dote on him before he left for work. The two cooks sulked, fearing for their jobs, but Gini was bored with her role of doing nothing.

"Money is wasted on some people," Felicia jeered silkily the first morning she discovered Gini in the kitchen in her jeans and apron scrambling eggs for Jordan.

"Would you care to join us for breakfast, Felicia?" Gini had asked simply.

"I'd prefer a French omelette," Felicia had replied, "the way Chole does them."

"Then you'll have to rustle up Chole for that." Oh, she was changing in some mysterious way, becoming more independent, less willing to allow herself to be bullied, Gini realized in surprise.

"I haven't the time," Felicia retorted.

On the beach Gini made friends with the famous and the rich as readily as she'd once made friends among the teachers and students in Clear Lake.

Felicia informed her coldly, "You invade people's privacy when you wave and speak to them so openly here at Malibu, Gini. There are unwritten rules out here that you'll have to learn we all abide by. You'll be an embarrassment to Jordan if you don't. These people are important. They'll nod if they want to see you and walk past you if they don't."

"I don't want to bother with stupid games like that," Gini had answered. "I'm already an embarrassment. I'll speak to everyone I see."

"They'll cut you dead and despise you."

But they didn't. It was amazing how soon these important people came to look forward to pausing and exchanging a few words with this sweet young woman who wanted nothing from them except the brief pleasure of their companionship.

James Storme, who was renowned for never recognizing anyone on the beach, even starlets in string bikinis, was constantly at Gini's side when she took her afternoon walks, a fact Jordan deeply resented. Jordan grew even angrier when Gini refused to abandon her new friendship with James.

"I can *talk* to James. He's like a brother," Gini attempted to explain, asserting herself with her newfound independence.

"Some brother," Jordan grumbled. "You're probably the only woman in L.A. so taken with his brotherly instincts."

"But he's nice to me. Trust me, Jordan. What does it hurt to take a walk now and then on a public beach with a man who happens to be our next-door neighbor?"

"Nothing, I guess, as long as you come home to me."

She had laughed, soft laughter tinged with desire. "Silly, who else would I come home to?"

Jordan had kissed her then, his mouth fierce and demanding, his arms crushing her to him, and James was instantly forgotten in the violent tidal wave of passion that swept them.

The press besieged Gini. They seemed determined to provoke her into another tantrum, and when no fresh outburst was forthcoming, her silence was used against her. The headlines grew more and more terrible. Journalists editorialized endlessly about what a mismatched couple she and Jordan were. There was much speculation about the disastrous effect she could have on his career.

One article, with a picture of Gini walking beside James, especially infuriated Jordan.

Jordan looked past every innuendo that appeared in print about her except for references to her friendship with James Storme. Felicia was not so kindly inclined and even went so far as to say Gini was becoming a publicity liability. More than once Gini heard Jordan defending her to his business manager.

Despite Gini's small successes and her new boldness in standing up for herself, she was deeply conscious of the effect all this publicity was having. She grew more and more convinced that she could never fit into Jordan's life. Jordan canceled a tour he'd been planning for the next spring, and this decision brought with it even more tension.

Felicia was livid, and she blamed Gini for Jordan's decision, telling her that even Louie and Wolf disliked her because Jordan no longer seemed as vitally interested in his music. Everyone was sure the fans were going to resent her for coming between Jordan and his music.

"I know Jordan is trying to make this ridiculous relationship work," Felicia had whispered one afternoon when she found Gini alone. "But I'm sure he realizes he's fighting a losing battle. Whether you'll admit it or not, you're ruining him."

Gini endured Felicia's awful confidences because she believed it better to know what Felicia was thinking than not to know.

But even if Gini was detrimental to Jordan's career, if she was failing to be the glamorous kind of woman everyone expected a star's wife to be, Melanie was blossoming at Malibu. For once she had two parents to love her and enough money so that she no longer felt insecure. Jordan spent as much time as he could with his daughter. He even helped her with the composition of a song she'd been working on for over a year, promising that they would record it together. Gini was beginning to learn to live with her daughter's fascination for rock music because she saw that there was no unwholesome aspect to Jordan's career.

The people Gini met on the beach were basically family oriented. Melanie was quickly finding acceptance with their children. They began to invite her places. Jordan's parents showered Melanie with gifts and took her sightseeing.

Melanie was making a new life for herself, even if her mother wasn't sure she would ever succeed in doing so. And though Gini was pleased, in a way Melanie's happiness only put Gini under more pressure, making it harder to decide whether she should stay with Jordan or return to Texas in the fall.

One afternoon Gini was walking with James on the beach.

James paused to let her catch up to his long strides. "Gini, have you thought any more about what you might do if you stay out here?" The wind was in his blond hair.

She frowned. "Only a little, but I mailed my signed contract back to Clear Lake this morning."

"Does Jordan know?" There was genuine concern in his deep voice.

"Not yet. But I just don't think things are working out, James."

"Jordan seems happy enough."

"He's trying very hard."

"Because he loves you."

"Maybe because he loves Melanie. How can he keep wanting me when everyone hates me? They think I'm coming between Jordan and his music. I just don't fit in, James."

"Hell. Who does? Find something to do, and that won't matter anymore. You'll have made a place for yourself without even trying to."

"There is something," she began, "that I might like to try. But it's so ridiculous. I mean, I have no experience. No talent." In her excitement, she had stopped walking.

"Don't sell yourself short. What is it?"

"I've been thinking about all the visual aids I had to use when I was teacher. Most of them were terrible. I've been remembering things I needed to supplement my teaching, but they just weren't available. Oh, this is going to sound so silly, but how do you learn to make a film, James? For kids and teachers?''

Suddenly he roared with laughter. A starlet pranced by, in a bikini the size of three postage stamps. James didn't even see her. He only saw Gini. "I knew I should have been wary when you boldly climbed up to my porch. You're out here two weeks, and you want to make movies. Gini, don't worry another minute about not fitting in. You're just like all the rest of us, whether you know it or not."

"Seriously, James."

"I've never been more serious in my life, dear child. Get a catalogue from UCLA for starters. I've got a few books. There are some people I know—"

"I'll borrow a book or two, but I'm not ready for the people you know."

Jordan stepped out onto the loggia. The beach was almost deserted, but his black gaze found Gini and James instantly. Jordan's stomach tightened at the sight of James' lean form bent attentively to Gini.

It galled Jordan that Gini had made friends with James Storme of all people. Jordan was sure that friendship was the last thing on Storme's mind. Not that Jordan blamed Storme, the way Gini looked so pretty with her wind-tossed curls, with her sweet smile and lovely big eyes. Gini leaned forward and whispered something to James. There was an intensity about her manner that upset Jordan. His brown hands clenched the railing. Then he called down to her.

Gini looked up, and her pretty face lit with a radiance that made her even more glowingly beautiful. Jordan swallowed his jealousy. "Gini, you haven't forgotten Clay and Fawna are coming to dinner, have you?''

Gini had already said her goodbyes and was halfway up the stairs. "No, I haven't forgotten," she murmured.

"I'm surprised you have time for your walk."

"It's amazing what a girl with two maids and two cooks has time for."

"I want this dinner to be special."

"Oh, it will be. Chole is absolutely exhausted. And did you see the way I decorated your forest?"

"Clay and I go back a long way. He says Fawna is different from the vacuous starlets he's married in the past. If he's right, it would be great if you two could be friends. She's new out here, too."

Before Jordan could say anything more he knew the sweetness of Gini's lips on his, of her fingertips ruffling his hair playfully.

She smiled shyly, blushing at her boldness, and tried to draw away, but his hunger to have her, whetted by his jealousy, had risen in him and he wouldn't let her go.

"If you make time for Storme, you can make time for me," he said gruffly, forgetting Clay and Fawna.

Gini had learned not to counter any comment he made regarding James. She mercly laughed softly and nuzzled his cheek. His lips moved to her throat, and she shivered involuntarily at their burning intensity. He lifted her into his arms.

Fawna was unconventionally beautiful in the conventional Hollywood way. Long, wild, dye-bottle-black curls framed her exquisite face. She had dark slanting eyes. They too were wild. They reminded Gini of a panther's eyes. These eyes sought Jordan too frequently for Gini to feel entirely comfortable around her.

Fawna's magnicent hourglass figure was squeezed into a tight leather sheath that was slit to the thigh. She dominated the dinner party with a stream of continuous Hollywood gossip when she wasn't talking about herself and her ambitions as an actress.

In a simple yellow sundress and heels, Gini felt quite ordinary. Not that she envied Fawna. Gini actually thought she might like her—in small doses, if Fawna would quit being such a flirt. There was something about her that almost made Gini glad to be ordinary.

Clay was a comedian with a string of successful movies. He had been Jordan's best friend ever since Jordan had moved to the West Coast. Clay seemed content to let Fawna do all the talking. Jordan had told Gini that Fawna was Clay's fourth wife, and that in the early stages of Clay's marriages he was usually so besotted that he gave in to his wives on every issue.

Gini discovered Fawna had been in one of Clay's movies. He had wanted her, and she had seen the advantages to marrying a famous movie star, so they'd run off to Vegas and married with a fanfare of publicity.

Fawna and Clay had just returned from a month-long honeymoon at Clay's castle in Scotland. When asked about the trip, Fawna confided in Gini, "Clay loved it. He read scripts, holed up in his room and meditated for a week and then worked on the characterization of his next role. But if you ask me, I'll take California warmth and sunshine over that dreary place any day. I nearly died of boredom. There were no people, no parties, no shops. I'm not into rain."

"Scottish mist, dear," Clay corrected mildly.

"They'd call Noah's flood a Scottish mist. The weather's really quite nasty. And so-o-o-o cold. I completely lost my all-over tan." Fawna glanced flirtatiously toward Jordan.

"I've always wanted to go to Scotland," Gini said wistfully. "But I could never afford to travel."

"Well, sounds like you're going to get your wish, since Jordan's leased Clay's castle for six weeks this summer," Fawna said.

"What?" Gini stared across the room at Jordan in surprise.

"Oh, my. Isn't he taking you, dear?" There wasn't a trace of sympathy in Fawna's voice. Only speculative interest.

"Of course I'm taking her," Jordan snapped. He got up and came over to sit down beside Gini. He took her hand in his. "I was going to tell you, Gini," he said casually. "Soon. I want to use Clay's castle for the location of my new video. It's just that I never like to talk about projects I'm trying to hash out."

"Does that mean you won't be giving your annual party on July Fourth, Jordan?" Clay asked mildly.

"Probably we won't. I really think it would be too much for Gini to try to manage a party on such short notice, especially when we'll be leaving right afterward," Jordan replied, reaching out and curving his arm around Gini's shoulders.

"I could try, Jordan, if it's something you've always done," Gini said, "even though I've never given a big party before."

"I don't see why she couldn't manage it," Fawna said knowledgeably to Jordan. "If you hire the right people, they do everything. Clay and I are going to give a party soon...." Fawna began, in what turned out to be an endless gush of words that nobody paid any attention to.

Later over after-dinner drinks, the subject of Fawna's conversation became Gini. "You're not at all what anyone expected, dear. You're really quite...quite..." For once Fawna stalled, at a loss for words.

"I know what you mean," Gini said quietly. The dinner party had only made her more aware than ever of how awkwardly she fit into Jordan's life.

"Well, I don't." Jordan was genuinely annoyed. "If you think I want some brainless starlet for a wife..." He stopped himself in time, not wishing to insult Clay, but if Clay really thought Fawna any different from the other three mistakes he'd made, Clay was definitely crazy where women were concerned.

Fawna leaped on the word "starlet." "Many starlets are aspiring to be serious actresses, Jordan. Me, for one, and I'm also a singer. I've even written a song or two that might interest you." She leaned forward to pick up her drink as if to emphasize the point she was making, and deliberately she let her breasts spill enticingly against her low-cut leather bodice. She stared up at Jordan seductively through downcast false eyelashes.

Since Fawna was right in front of him, Jordan could hardly avoid looking at her vast expanse of exposed bosom. He flushed darkly and leaned back against the couch.

Suddenly the evening was simply too much for Gini. "Excuse me, please. I'm really not feeling at all well." She jerked free the hand Jordan had been absently holding and ran stumbling out onto the loggia. Jordan was right behind her.

Lightning blinked on the horizon. A strong wind tumbled white waves high upon the deserted beach.

"Jordan, it's no use." Gini's voice was full of tears.

"What, darling?" Cautiously he reached out to touch her arm. She wrenched away from him.

"Us. No matter how hard I try, I just don't belong out here. Fawna would hop in bed with her husband's best friend without giving it a thought. If you think I could ever be friends with someone like Fawna..."

Jordan reached out and pulled her into his arms, holding her so tightly she could hardly breathe. "I wouldn't want you to be," he said softly, his voice muffled in her hair.

"But Clay," she began in a small voice, her eyes glistening. She tipped her head back to gaze at his face. The warmth of his breath fanned her cheeks.

"Forget Clay," he commanded gently. "Fawna is his problem, not ours."

"You said tonight was important." Her hand moved against his crisp shirt, coming to rest upon his chest. She could feel the steady drumbeat of his heart beneath her hand.

"Because he told me Fawna was special. But she's even worse than his other wives."

"I couldn't stand the way she kept looking at you."

"She'd look at anyone she thinks might be able to advance her career. Tonight should have shown you how much I need you, Gini, not that you don't fit in. Hell, if you don't stay with me, I'll end up with a Fawna who wants me only for what I can do for her."

Nothing else he could have said could have pleased her more. Gini met his gaze and smiled, her face softly aglow in the darkness. "Why didn't you tell me about Scotland before?" she whispered.

"I wanted to be sure about it before I told you."

"When would that have been?"

"Tonight, after I'd finalized the arrangements with Clay. It'll only take about ten days to shoot the footage for the video, and that's even if it rains every other day. After that I thought it would be nice to be away from this madhouse. Just the two of us. There won't be any reporters."

Something warm and intimately disarming had come into his voice. She thought of being alone with him in the wildness of Scotland. Her heart skipped a beat, then refused to return to an even rhythm.

"Would Felicia be there?" she asked.

Her hand was engulfed in the largeness of his.

"Felicia said she'd fly up from London for a day when we're filming. My parents want to take Melanie to Hawaii for a month so she can get to know their other granddaughter; after all, they are first cousins. Then they'll come over, too. You and I would be alone for a few weeks, Gini. It would be almost like a honeymoon."

"Not like Fawna and Clay's, I hope?"

He laughed softly and drew her more closely against him. "I'm not into meditating."

"What are you into?" An impish gleam had come into her eyes.

"You," he replied huskily.

She had begun to tremble. "Jordan, it looks like it's going to rain." She leaned against him, and he caressed the nape of her neck with his index finger. "I love walking in the rain. Why don't we go down to the beach?"

He tenderly took her hand and brought it to his lips. He blew a warm kiss through her fingers. Slowly his hot gaze touched her eyes, her mouth, and then moved lower, stripping her. "I'll just go inside and speak to Clay," he murmured. "Then I'll be back with a couple of raincoats."

A few minutes later he returned and helped her into an overlarge raincoat. Together they climbed down to the beach. The water was higher than Gini had ever seen it, coming almost to the houses. A brisk wind had come up, and cobwebs of lightning zigzagged crazily beneath ink-black clouds. Thunder crashed.

The storm infected them with excitement, and they ran along the beach, even letting the water curl around their shoes. It began to rain, suddenly, violently, great spattering droplets, and Jordan drew Gini beneath the deck of a house, where they stood, holding hands, watching as the rain blew in fierce gusts across the beach.

The rain dripped from the house and splashed onto Gini's collar, trickling down her neck like icy fingers. She shivered, and Jordan pulled her into his arms.

"You must be freezing," he declared with velvet huskiness. "Maybe this wasn't such a good idea."

Plastic raincoats crinkled. Her senses were pleasantly assaulted by his musky male scent and the warmth of his body heat. She felt warmed as though she stood near a roaring fire.

"I think it was a very good idea," she said in an amused, slightly breathless voice.

"Do you?" He ran his fingers through her hair, smoothing the damp curls. With his hands he framed her face, his thumbs caressing her chin in hypnotically sensuous circles. He tilted her chin.

Through half-closed lashes, Gini gazed up at him, and her pulse leaped as she saw his eyes lingering upon her mouth.

"Kiss me," she whispered. Her eyes rested calmly and steadily on his face. In the near darkness her eyes were immense pools of glowing blackness. Her lush lips parted invitingly.

"Anything to oblige a lady." He brought her even closer. He tipped her head back and lowered his mouth to hers. His deepening kiss ignited a searing white-hot blaze of desire within her. His lips moved to her throat, his tongue scalding against her skin. A long quiver rippled the length of her body. She swayed against the solid wall of his chest. Her hands wrapped around his neck in fierce possession.

"Jordan. Oh, Jordan." How would she ever manage to live without him again?

His hunger was as insatiable as hers. He shaped her feminine form to the hard contours of his male body. She strained closer, her heart hammering as wildly as the thunder of the storm.

"If only things could work out between us, Jordan. I would be so happy." Her voice was a soft, agonized whisper from deep in her throat.

His hand smoothed damp, waving tendrils of hair from her face. "They'll work out, if only you'll stop fighting yourself and me."

"I'm not fighting you now."

He kissed her again, and she felt shocks of fiery sensation where his lips touched her. For a timeless moment they were oblivious to the raging storm. They were aware only of each other.

The rushing wind howled with more fury, whistling eerily in the eaves, pushing against them and carrying the huge black thunderheads swiftly over the crashing waves of the Pacific toward them. Lightning flashed and turned the turbulent waters a shimmering white. Thunder was an incessant low rumble.

"I think we'd better run for home," Jordan muttered reluctantly at last. He grabbed her hand and pulled her along as they ran eagerly back to his mansion. The rain was falling in torrents. By the time they managed the scramble up the slick rocks and stairs, they were both drenched.

They ran laughing to their bedroom. Jordan went into the bathroom to get some towels. Gini walked out onto the private sun deck to watch the storm from this sheltered porch.

The fierce wind whipped her raincoat and blew rain all over her. She was so cold her teeth were chattering. She went back inside and closed the glass door behind her.

Both her hands were plunged deeply into the pockets of her raincoat. In the right pocket her fingers closed over a wadded bit of lacy fabric. Curious, she withdrew the object and unfolded it.

It was a tiny, delicately embroidered handkerchief. Lingering traces of a vaguely familiar scent clung to it. Gini turned it over on her palm. The name Felicia had been carefully embroidered across the center of the white square. She caught a whiff of the perfume again. Lilacs.

Once not long ago, Felicia must have borrowed Jordan's raincoat. Had they walked on the rainswept beach together? Had they come back and made love?

Gini's teeth were no longer chattering. She had forgotten the cold. Her feeling of light-hearted joy had fled. Her thrill to the wildness of the storm had vanished as well. Was she just another in a long line of women—the only difference being that she had once been married to Jordan and given birth to his child?

Numbly, she replaced the handkerchief in the pocket and then tore the coat from her body.

Jordan strode back into the bedroom, his muscled chest bare, his black hair sexily tousled from being towel dried.

Her pulse throbbed jerkily as he lazily approached her. Minus his shirt, he exuded an aura of male virility. Pain splintered through her nerves at the thought of him with Felicia.

He came up to her and began to ruffle her hair with a towel until the soft curls were merely damp. Stiffly she endured his nearness.

"Something's wrong again," he said in a low, insistent voice.

She tried to move away from him. "I just want to be left alone now," she said.

His fingers closed around the soft flesh of her upper arm. "Left alone? After leading me on down there on the beach—"

Something snapped inside her. "I didn't lead you on."

"You damn sure weren't acting like you are now."

"I'm sorry for the way I acted then."

"An apology for your behavior on the beach is the last thing I want. It's the way you're acting now I don't like."

"Then I'm sorry for that," she countered stiffly.

"I want you to stop swinging from hot to cold. Every time you act like this I think you're going to walk out on me, and I go through the hell of losing you all over again. Damn it, Gini, just this once, tell me what's wrong."

"I found Felicia's handkerchief in the pocket of the raincoat you lent me. I know she was the woman you were involved with before you came to Houston and found me again."

She had turned away from him, but Jordan could see her reflection in the sliding glass door.

Jordan's lips tightened. "And?"

"I keep thinking she'd be much better for you than I could ever be."

"Damn it. I don't want Felicia. Our relationship was her idea in the first place, not mine. And it wasn't working."

"She's so beautiful, so glamorous, and she loves you."

"She was like all the rest of the women I've known since you. And to set the record straight—she never loved me. She was merely protecting her investment by becoming personally involved with me. It was a convenient relationship, for both of us. That's all. It's over now. So forget the handkerchief and Felicia. Let's get back to where we were."

"Just like that?"

"Just like this." His husky voice held anger but sensuality as well. His hand reached out and gently touched her neck.

"How can I?" she asked, trying to pull away.

He held her fast, his fingers lingering possessively.

"I'll show you."

"Jordan. No!"

Her rejection shattered his control. He seized her by the shoulders, his grip hard and painful. His handsome face was savage with pain and with some other powerful, unreadable emotion. "It's always no, even when you really mean yes, isn't it? Do you know what that does to me?"

"Jordan—"

"Shut up!"

Gini strained against his hold. His answer was to jerk her onto her tiptoes. "You drive me crazy. I don't know what you want, what to do to make you happy. I'd do anything, Gini. Anything."

"Then let me go."

"I'm through listening to you. Just this once I'm going to make myself happy for a change." His fingers circled her throat. His mouth came down hard and angry on her lips, bruising their softness. "Just this once..." he muttered thickly.

He kissed her long and deeply in a barbaric kiss that made her forget everything except her need of him. His lips played roughly over hers, eating at her lips, her tongue, devouring the soft warm insides of her mouth. He held her against his lean, hard body and she felt the taut pressure of his aroused state against her thighs. He was shaking, so fierce was his need. Beneath her exploring fingertips he felt on fire. His desire was so blatant that a quiver that was both fear and ecstasy melted down Gini's spine.

Tentatively her hands circled his broad shoulders. Felicia was forgotten. There was only Jordan. Only his anger and his passion. Only hot, blistering lips that washed all doubt from her mind. Only two bodies, two souls on fire with the same need.

Minutes later he lifted her into his arms and carried her to the bed. Quickly he undressed her and then he stripped out of his own clothes. Her dress and his slacks lay in a damp, tangled heap on the carpet, at the foot of the bed.

Jordan lowered his sun-browned body on top of hers once more. His hand slipped between her thighs to enjoy the feel of velvety skin. Expert fingers touched, rubbed and played with the sensitive perfumed flesh. All too soon Gini's emotions reeled out of control, and she clung to him, moaning softly at the soaring pleasure burning through her shaking body.

The silence of the room, breathlessly hushed, remained unbroken except for the whispered sounds of passion from the bed. Jordan made love to every part of her body, raining kisses into her hair, upon her forehead, her cheeks, her throat, her breasts, and lower, upon the soft curve of her belly, the dewy sweetness of her rose petal womanhood, yet always returning lingeringly to her eager lips, taking her breath away with each fiery kiss.

He kissed each of her breasts, his mouth closing over one nipple at a time, biting softly, pulling gently with teasing teeth, and Gini was paralyzed by the electric response that jolted through her.

"Take me," she whispered.

His body slid against hers, and she knew the ecstasy of his fierce possession as he buried himself inside her. With a faint little whimper, she cried out. She looked into his eyes and saw they had gone dark with desire. As he began to move, Gini's world exploded on a blazing sensual flame that was all-enveloping. The tantalizing delight seemed to go on endlessly like a rippling current of spiraling flame.

Abruptly, his passion surged out of control, and he lost himself in the urgent demands of his own body, carrying Gini with him to rapturous paradise.

Afterward, Gini lay quietly beneath Jordan's sweat-sheened body. His dark face was buried against her throat. She felt too overwhelmed with delicious lassitude to speak. She merely stroked her fingers through the rich ebony of his hair and drowsily watched the storm that raged outside.

After a little while, Jordan's body grew uncomfortably heavy upon hers, but when she tried to push him away, she found that he had fallen asleep. He lay on top of her, his breath soft and warm as it caressed her neck. When she tried to shift herself away from him, his tanned fingers merely gripped her all the more tightly, and at last she, too, fell asleep.

She awoke to the feel of his maleness once more filling her, to the urgency of his wanting her, to her own need that was as fierce as his. Once more they surrendered to the warm succulent lure of one another, his fevered lips roaming her body until their desire raged out of control.

At last they were satisfied, and afterward they were consumed by a luscious weariness. They curled their bodies against one another and slept together, as tightly joined in sleep as they had been in love.

Ten

Mrs. Jacks, you must sit still,'' Roland demanded in exasperation.

"I'm sorry." Gini was trying very hard to sit quietly as Roland feathered the last vital touches on her face with his makeup brush, but she was so nervous about the party it was practically impossible.

Oh, why had she let Felicia talk her into having a professional makeup artist do her face right before the party? For that matter, why had she let Felicia talk her into the party, period?

It was only because Felicia had insinuated Jordan hadn't mentioned the party sooner because he didn't think she could give one. After that Gini had had to prove to everyone, especially Jordan, that she could do it. It was important that she star in some arena in his life other than their bedroom.

But what had she proven? Felicia had ended up planning the entire affair because Gini lacked the confidence to stick to her decisions when Felicia argued with her.

As Roland extended the black liner along one eye, Gini reread Melanie's postcard from Hawaii. At least Melanie was having a wonderful time with her cousin and grandparents.

"There," Roland said, tucking his brush away.

"At last!" Gini jumped up.

"Don't you even want to look into the mirror?" Roland cried in dismay, unaccustomed to such a lack of vanity in his clients.

"Oh, yes." She reached dutifully for his hand mirror.

An exotic, sophisticated creature with wild brown curls and slanting almond eyes smiled back at Gini from the mirror. She scarcely recognized herself. She felt almost like Cinderella on the night of the ball.

"It's wonderful," she murmured gratefully, wondering if it really was. "No one will ever know it's me."

Roland beamed, his ego soothed by the balm of her praise.

The party was to begin at six, and Gini thought she should talk to the caterer, Mr. Dumond, one last time. She murmured a few more words of thanks to Roland and then went downstairs where caterers rushed about stringing bright lights and American flags from tree limbs in the living room, setting up lanterns on the tented terraces by the pool, and draping banquet tables with red-and-white linen cloths. The party had a July Fourth theme.

Gini found Felicia and Mr. Dumond deep in conversation. It was obvious from Mr. Dumond's frown that Felicia was issuing a stream of instructions as the two of them inspected silver platters overflowing with diminutive pizzas, morsels of fillet on toast rounds, tiny leek tarts, bite-size quiches, and broiled chicken wings.

Gini hid behind the trees and watched them. As always when Felicia was present, Gini felt as if she were the guest and Felicia the proper hostess. Even this party had turned out to be Felicia's and not hers.

Jordan had been locked in his study all day working on a new song. He'd come out only for a quick lunch with Gini on the sun deck and a swim in the pool.

Deciding there was little point in talking to Mr. Dumond herself, Gini went upstairs to dress. She was still in her robe when Jordan came out of his study. He had showered and changed, but his eyes were weary from the long hours of work. In his hand he held a box tied with red ribbons. He came up and handed it to her, kissing her gently on the brow.

The box had a cellophane lid glassing the most exquisite ivory orchid Gini had ever seen. She stared at the flower, and then her gaze slowly rose to his.

"Why, Jordan, it's beautiful," she murmured with astonished pleasure.

"No more than you." His voice was gentle, and his eyes were so intense his look consumed her. "I'll be glad when this is over and you can stop being such a bundle of nerves." His expression changed. Brown fingers lifted her chin and inspected her more closely. "What have you done to yourself?"

She flushed expectantly.

"You look different," he said, his voice guarded.

"Only different?" She felt mildly deflated. She batted her long, curled doll's lashes. The sensitive Roland would have been appalled.

Jordan smiled in amusement. "You're lovely, of course, but I prefer the way you usually look."

She tossed her wild curls and tried to slither like a siren. "I was trying to look like a movie-star wife."

His arm slid around her waist and he drew her against his body. "How many times do I have to tell you, the last thing I want is a movie-star wife. I just want you."

He leaned down to kiss her, but before his lips touched hers, she jumped away.

"You'll ruin my lip gloss," she whispered in explanation.

"See what I mean," he said mockingly. "I like you better when you're kissable."

"That will be right after the party," she replied pertly.

"At least that'll give me something to look forward to tonight."

"So this whole extravaganza is wasted on you?"

"That's what I've been trying to tell you for weeks, Gini."

"You always give this party. I just didn't want you to change your life-style because of me."

"Not even when I want to change it? I only hope that after you've endured one of Felicia's circuses, you won't regret having done so. Open your present, Gini, or I'll think you don't like it."

Beneath his smiling gaze she ripped into the box. With trembling fingers she touched one of the velvet green leaves. The petals blurred in a mist of emotion.

As always, any attention from Jordan moved her deeply. Her luminous eyes met his, but before she could express her delight in the thoughtfulness of his gift, there was a knock at their door.

Felicia, beautiful in black silk and sequins, came in.

Jordan's arms fell from Gini's waist. "All set, Felicia?"

"I need you downstairs, Jordan." Her brisk tone held command. "Some of your guests have arrived, and the president of Astro Records would like a private word with you about your reasons for canceling your tour." She glanced darkly toward Gini at the mention of the canceled tour.

"All right," Jordan murmured, not seeming to mind Felicia's proprietary manner as she took his hand and led him down to the party.

Gini watched them leave, and as always when they were together, her heart filled with despair. They seemed so right for each other. Felicia was able to anticipate his every need and satisfy it. Felicia knew how to enhance his career. She wasn't threatened by it. She gloried in everything that intimidated Gini.

No matter how ardently Jordan proclaimed he loved Gini and not Felicia, Gini could never quite believe him, because she couldn't quite believe in herself.

Gini stared down at the exquisite white blossoms in the box, but her joy in his gift was gone. What did it mean, after all? He would have made the same romantic gesture toward any woman.

Gini finished dressing in silence. Then she pinned the orchid onto her white sundress and stepped out onto the sun deck where she could hear the music and the laughter drifting up from the terraces.

The party had started without her. Would she even be missed if she stayed in her room?

When she finally went down, the party was well under way. The house was brilliant with a shifting mass of glittery people. Felicia and Jordan were nowhere to be seen. Gini moved inconspicuously through the throng of people and slipped into a hidden niche behind a clump of trees in Felicia's indoor forest. From her corner she could watch the dancers.

James Storme's deep voice came from behind her. "Hiding, Gini?"

She whirled guiltily. Was she so obvious? The pale, frothy shawl she'd worn over her arms fell to the floor. She watched as James leaned down and retrieved it. He replaced it about her arms.

"You mustn't fly off now, just because I've come." He pulled out a pack of cigarettes and shook a few loose, offering her one. After she refused, he lit his own.

"Two actresses who've read the script of my next movie are pursuing me," he said.

"And I thought you'd come over here out of brotherly kindness," she said.

He laughed. "Hardly. I'm surprised Jordan hasn't set you straight about my character."

"Oh, he's tried."

"Brotherly kindness is not one of my virtues."

The music stopped and then resumed with a crash of drums. It was one of Jordan's hit songs, and it had a fierce, animal-wild beat. A spotlight came on, and Gini turned and saw Felicia in her glittering black gown as she led Jordan onto the dance floor into the circle of light. Not that he looked as if he minded. He was laughing down at the golden woman as she undulated seductively in her skintight sheath to the pulsing drumbeats. A ring of clapping spectators formed around them when Jordan began to dance too.

They were a striking couple, and they danced expertly together. Everyone had stopped talking to watch them. Jordan moved with pantherlike grace. Felicia was a dazzling whirl of flashing sequins as she twirled close to Jordan and then retreated, deliberately trying to tantalize him.

She came close again and grabbed the end of his tie. There was a wanton invitation in her brilliant eyes. Gini couldn't help noticing how perfectly they danced together. Just as she couldn't help noting how cynical eyebrows lifted with speculative knowledge. She felt she was dying inside.

The song went on, endlessly. Or did it only seem they would dance forever to that mad, frenzied tempo? Abruptly it was over, and Felicia collapsed into Jordan's arms, her hair spilling in a shower of gold over his shoulder.

"You mustn't mind that so very much, Gini," James said gently. "Every year Felicia has the spotlight and dances with him to that song. It's a tradition."

Gini gave a little shaken laugh. How could she fit into this blasé world where spectacles like that one were nothing to worry about?

At length James spoke. He had taken her hand in his. "Dear girl, that was a public display. Not genuine emotion. That's all he and Felicia ever had. That's all Felicia wanted. It wasn't enough for Jordan. Can't you understand? She wants Jordan the star. She wants to be seen with him, to be admired, to be envied and to be talked about. You love Jordan the man. You don't want to parade your feelings for him, because they're too private to be shared. That's why he wants you back. You're the only honest thing in his life besides his music."

Gini took a big breath and squeezed his hand tightly. "You are very kind and very brotherly, James, whether you admit it or not."

"Don't tell anyone, or you'll ruin my reputation."

"It will be our secret," she whispered. She reached on tiptoe and brushed his cheek with a sisterly kiss.

Jordan's cool voice came from above them. At the sound of it, Gini jerked her head sharply.

"So there you are, Gini!" His arms wrapped her waist, asserting possession. He forced a smile and said, "James, I should have known better than to invite you. Why don't you go let one of your starlets catch you?" Jordan's manner was deliberately jovial, and yet Gini knew he really wasn't joking.

"Heaven forbid," James replied dryly, but he took the hint and left them to rejoin the party, and the next time Gini saw him, he looked very bored indeed. The voluptuous Fawna was clinging to his arm and talking nonstop.

When James had gone, Jordan murmured against Gini's ear, "What took you so long to come down?"

His warm breath tingled. She shuddered in aching awareness of him as a man, despising herself for being so vulnerable to him.

"I was scared," she said in a stiff, tentative voice.

He traced the tip of her nose with a fingertip. Her heart fluttered beneath his intense, possessive gaze.

"Scared?" he asked kindly. "Oh, I guess anyone would be the first time. But you shouldn't be."

"I don't feel I belong."

The coldness in her manner was beginning to affect him. "That again. You're my wife."

"Not anymore."

"Name the day."

"Oh, Jordan. It's not that simple."

"For me it is." He swept her onto the dance floor. He held her fiercely, controlling his sudden anger. "Are you going to make me wait forever?"

"People are watching us," she whispered.

He only held her more tightly, pressing her into his virile body so that the fluid contours of hard muscle etched themselves into her flesh. She was feverishly conscious of the potent power of his masculinity.

"Let them," he murmured, bending his head to hers.

"I can't dance like Felicia."

"That's the last thing I want."

"You seemed to be enjoying yourself immensely with her a while ago."

"That was Felicia's idea."

"But you went along with it."

"I couldn't find you." His lips were in her hair against her earlobe. "Look, Gini, that meant nothing."

"To me it did."

"Darling, I'm sorry."

"You are so sexy with her." Her whisper was almost painful.

"I felt like I was on stage. I was putting on an act. Living up to my image. Being an entertainer. That was all."

Was the image the real Jordan? Or was the man before her?

He lifted his head away from hers so that he could stare down into her face. Was it the tender persuasion in his vivid eyes that made her feel so breathless, or was it the dancing? Whatever, he was utterly irresistible. She tore her gaze from his and fought to concentrate on the third button of his shirt.

"If you want me to fire Felicia I will, Gini, though it will cost me a fortune to break my contract, and she's good at what she does."

"Oh, I can see...she's very enthusiastic about her work."

"Stop it. I'm not interested in her as a woman, and I'll never dance with her again if that upsets you."

"That isn't the only thing that upsets me."

"Gini, I want you to quit stalling and make a commitment to me. The summer's going fast."

Her heart was beating in her throat. They whirled in a series of quick turns. A potted tree swirled past, a group of studio executives, a golden woman in black sequins.

Felicia.

She was staring into Gini's eyes. Gini looked straight at her and gave her a brilliant smile. Felicia's brows arched. She was taken aback by such boldness. Then she smiled too, slowly, triumphantly.

For the rest of the evening Gini would not be able to erase Felicia's cool, triumphant smile from her mind no matter how she tried.

When the music stopped, Jordan and Gini were on the opposite end of the room from Felicia and beside the long windows that looked over the pool and the Pacific. People were staring at them, some of the women with open curiosity, some with a touch of malicious envy or disdain as they noted every detail of Gini's appearance.

Jordan held Gini by the hand in an iron grip so that she could not escape. A famous rock star waved to Jordan from across the room. A beautiful woman in red satin jeans smiled warmly at him.

"Jordan, you don't have to bother with me. Visit with your friends," Gini pleaded. "Felicia has invited so many important people. I'm sure they want to see you."

"Don't be such a little idiot," he retorted, sweeping her onto the floor again.

"I'm afraid I'm being a terrible influence as usual, making you neglect your duties as host. Felicia will be livid tomorrow."

"Do you really think I give a damn?"

He whirled her outside onto the loggia, where they slipped unnoticed into the darker shadows of the terrace. They stopped dancing, but he continued to hold her delicious warmth lightly in his arms.

The music throbbed in the background. Sweet-scented jasmine spilled from a trellis. Moonlight glimmered on the Pacific. The edge of her skirt was brushing against the velvet petals of a thick clump of potted geraniums.

She was conscious of his thumbs absently stroking the nape of her neck in silken circles that made her skin feel on fire. She shivered.

"Cold?" His hand slid partway down her bare back and he drew her more closely against the warmth of his body.

Mutely she shook her head though she trembled again. His merest touch sent sensuous ripples through her veins. She willed herself to ignore his gently massaging hand upon her spine, but it was impossible.

"I want you to tell me tonight, Gini, what you plan to do in the fall. I've tried to be patient, but I'm at the end of my rope. Your principal called the other day from Houston, and I found out you'd signed your teaching contract for next year. I keep waiting for you to tell me something, and you say nothing. You've even used planning this party to keep me at a distance. Every time I ask, you put me off."

"Because I don't know, Jordan." Her soft whisper held a world of pain.

"Damn it. Give me an answer. I want you so much. I can't go on wondering. I want everything resolved between us before we leave for Scotland."

"All right, Jordan. I'll make up my mind tonight. I promise, and I'll let you know right after the party's over. But I have to be alone for a little while, to think."

He hesitated. Someone called his name from the balcony above them, searching for him. "All right, Gini. I won't pressure you." He placed a gentle kiss on her tousled curls and left her to go upstairs.

After a little while Gini drifted back into the house. She wandered through the crush of people, who were all too absorbed with making an impression on one another to pay attention to her. Gini took a glass of champagne from a silver tray a waiter offered her and began to sip it. The party with its laughter and dancing went on around her, but she was no longer a part of it.

She was lost in her own thoughts. Should she stay with Jordan? If Jordan wanted her, did it really matter if she fit into his world perfectly? Maybe he really did need a wife who was completely outside all that.

Wasn't one stormy year with Jordan worth a lifetime of living alone? There was Melanie to consider. Jordan was a wonderful father.

Gini set her half-finished champagne flute down on the marble ledge of the fireplace. She would have to find Jordan and talk to him. Together they would decide.

He wasn't easily found. She searched everywhere, inside the house and out on the terraces, but he was gone. At last she asked Clay and Fawna.

Fawna ignored Clay's look of warning and said slyly, "Why don't you go down to the beach, Gini dear?"

"Oh, thank you, Fawna," Gini answered gratefully before she rushed outside, flying down the rough wooden stairs to the soft sand. At first the beach seemed deserted, so she wandered toward James's house.

Then she heard voices, and she froze.

A tall man and a woman were standing in the deep shadows near the rocks beneath a cluster of palm trees. They obviously wanted to be alone. Felicia's sequined gown flashed in the moonlight. A hot bolt of pain went through Gini. She had recognized the couple instantly.

Some instinct warned Gini not to call out to them. Then she heard her own name, and wild horses couldn't have dragged her away no matter how guilty she felt for eavesdropping.

"Jordan, Gini has had a disastrous impact on your image. You heard what Joe Simon said."

"Maybe I've outgrown the bachelor image."

"Jordan, you and I had something special together before she came. We could have it again if she was gone. If it's marriage you want, why her? Why not me? She hates the fact that you're a celebrity, and that's a vital part of you, Jordan, whether you admit it or not. She doesn't know the first thing about how to conduct herself with the press, about how to play up to the right people. She can't even give a party. Tonight would have been a bomb if I'd let her handle it. Worst of all, she doesn't even care."

"She cares. No one could adjust to living like this in a month, and especially not after what she's been through. It took me years."

"You were nothing when she was with you before. You were even satisfied with being nothing. She's ruining you, Jordan. How can I stand by and watch her destroy everything we've built together?"

"She loves *me*. You love what I am."

"Is that so wrong? Ask yourself this, Jordan, who has done more for you? Who can do more for you? I made you a star. Do you really want to throw that away?"

"No."

"Kiss me, Jordan, just one last time. Is it really so much better with her?"

In the silent darkness, Gini knew a pain more profound than any she'd ever known before. The surf rushed up, glimmering and wet, and kissed the sand lingeringly, only to be sucked back into the ocean once more. The wind rustled in the palm fronds, but Gini was aware only of the lengthening silence between the man and the woman in the nearby darkness. As Gini imagined Jordan's lips on Felicia's, his hands on her body, a tiny sob was wrenched from her throat. She whirled blindly and ran stumbling back inside the mansion.

Felicia had given Jordan stardom. What had Gini ever done for him? What *could* she do for him?

No matter what Jordan said, he wasn't like other men. He was a celebrity. She couldn't blame him for Felicia. She knew he'd fought as hard as she had to believe there was a chance for their marriage. The passion he felt for her was very real, but love and passion would never be enough to bridge the differences between them. Felicia was right. Even if Felicia didn't love him as Gini did, she could give him something he needed more than love. If Gini left, Jordan would eventually find happiness with Felicia.

She had to give Jordan up, just as she had all those years ago, and for the same reasons—because she could never be the kind of woman he really needed.

As Gini moved through the crowded room, laughing strangers jostled into her. Her lungs filled with the acrid scent of cigarette smoke. She caught the fragrance of expensive perfumes.

Across the room she saw James lounging indolently against the wall, a beautiful redhead standing beside him. A new song came on with a beat as wildly primitive as the one Felicia and Jordan had danced to.

Suddenly Gini realized she couldn't just run away again. Jordan was too stubborn to let her go so easily. She would have to do something to convince him he didn't want her anymore. Something so terrible there would be no question of his coming after her.

She caught James's quizzical gaze and held it. Then she knew what she had to do. Slowly her lips curved into an alluring smile that brought a dark look of surprise to

James's craggy male face as she made her way toward him. The starlet at his side, sensing competition, drifted away.

"Gini, what's wrong?" James asked. "You look like you've been crying."

"That's all over now. Everything's all over," she replied enigmatically. She grabbed the end of his tie and pulled his face down toward hers as she'd seen Felicia do when she danced with Jordan. Reaching forward seductively, she removed his glasses and put them into his pocket. She let her fingers linger upon his chest. "I can see why they say you're the sexiest man in Hollywood," she murmured.

"Hey. What's gotten into you?" James whispered, genuinely startled.

"Can't you even act like you think I'm sexy?"

"What?"

"You're the only person who can help me," she said in a low, desperate voice. "Because Jordan is so jealous of you. I'm leaving him, James, and I don't want him coming after me. I want you to dance with me the way he danced with Felicia."

"You want to use me to make Jordan jealous?"

"I hope it'll do more than that."

"He'll kill me."

"Sure, he'll get mad. I want him to get so mad he'll let me go. But he wouldn't resort to violence toward you, James. It's me he'll be furious with."

James looked skeptical.

"Aren't you my friend, James?"

"Why do I have the feeling I'm beginning to wish I wasn't?"

"Because you're going to help me."

He shrugged, smiling ruefully. The jungle beat of the music wrapped around them. "Something tells me they're playing our song."

"And after we dance, James, you're going to drive me to the airport in your fanciest car so we'll be sure to make the papers."

"You mean, if I get out of here alive."

"Don't worry. I'll protect you."

Gini pulled him by the tie out onto the center of the dance floor. They began to sway lazily to the wild, frenzied tempo of the music. People began to watch them. Gini was aware of the terrific power of James's animal magnetism, and even though she was immune to it, the other women watched James, mesmerized.

The straps of Gini's white dress fell from her shoulders to her arms, and she didn't bother to pull them up. The light shone in her hair, in her brilliant tawny eyes, and glimmered on the single gold chain that jumped against her trembling, half-exposed breasts. Her graceful body twirled, her silken skirts circling high to reveal her shapely legs. Not a man in the room could take his eyes off her.

There was passion in her dance, the wild blind passion of a woman who was so deeply in love she was willing to sacrifice her own happiness for that of her beloved. Her anguish and fire reached out and touched everyone's heart though they mistook James for the object of her love.

At just the moment when the dance reached a climax of frenzied drumbeats, Jordan came inside from the terrace. He was searching for Gini. His eyes were drawn to the couple dancing so sensuously together. In her pale clinging gown, she was a vision of youthful sensuality. He watched her body undulate rhythmically and remembered the way she moved beneath him in bed. Desire tore through him as savagely as a knife. With it was a low, smoldering anger more intense than anything he'd ever known.

The music stopped, and Gini leaned forward and kissed James, a long, smothering kiss. Storme's tall, lean body seemed molded to Gini's. Murderous hatred filled Jordan.

When Gini lifted her face, her golden-brown eyes searched the room for Jordan. When she found him, her gaze locked with his for a soul-destroying eternity. At last she ripped her eyes from his dark, anguished features. Then she took James's hand, and together they ran from the room.

Jordan plunged through the crowded room after them. In an instant his world had become an awful hell. Gini had deliberately humiliated him, she who never deliberately hurt anyone. Why?

Oh God, he'd been such a fool! He had believed her when she said Storme was only a friend. Was it possible that Gini was no different from all the other women who'd used him?

Jordan ran out into the darkness, past the ring of officers he'd hired for security. Reporters swarmed around him. Bulbs flashed to catch his private torment for the insatiable appetites of gossip-starved readers.

Questions bombarded him. Microphones were shoved in front of his face.

"Was that your ex-wife with James Storme?"

"Has she left you for him?"

Jordan pushed the man aside and ran toward James's house. Storme's garage door opened, and his gleaming sports car spun out. Gini was held tightly in James Storme's free arm.

"That's our answer, boys," a journalist yelled.

"It's sure as hell mine," Jordan snarled beneath his breath.

He hoped he would never see her again.

Eleven

There was no one in the VIP lounge but James and Gini.
They sat huddled together silently. James had to exercise
considerable restraint not to question her. Gini's thoughts
were filled with the terrible pain she'd seen on Jordan's
face as he watched her drive away with James. She would
carry his haunted expression with her for the rest of her
life.

Her makeup was smudged from tears and her own
carelessness at wiping at her eyes. Her pale features were
thin and drawn. Because she'd been cold in her flimsy, low-
cut dress, James had loaned her his coat. His coat sleeves
fell over Gini's wrists as she clutched her ticket to Houston, making her look like a little lost waif.

"You sure have style when you decide to give a guy his
walking papers," James said, breaking the silence. "Jordan must be more of a bastard than I ever realized. What
did he do to you?"

"Oh, James, you don't understand. He didn't do anything!"

"Nothing?"

"I love him." Suddenly she began to weep again.

He pulled her into his arms and smoothed her hair. "You have a strange way of showing it."

"But I do. I love him more than anyone in the world."

The door of the lounge crashed open, and Jordan stormed inside, his dark face still livid with fury. His black eyes blazed. In two strides he crossed the room and yanked Gini out of James's comforting embrace.

"You're not leaving me without an explanation," he growled.

"Jordan," Gini faltered. "I didn't think you'd want to see me again after I—"

He cut her off. "Neither did I."

"Jordan, I made my decision, and I'm leaving you."

"And I've made mine," he snarled. He picked her up and slung her over his right shoulder as if she were a sack of potatoes.

"Put me down," she yelled. She began to thrash wildly, her heels flying in the air. She balled her hands into fists and pounded against his shoulders and back.

Instead of complying he strode toward the door.

"James, you can't let him do this to me," she cried.

"Trust my brotherly instincts, Gini dear. And take care of my coat. I had it custom-made."

"James!" she screamed indignantly.

The minute Jordan stepped outside the lounge, reporters were everywhere.

"Somebody help me!" Gini hissed.

A short fat man grabbed Jordan by the arm.

"You can't treat her like that, Jacks, I don't care who you are."

"Butt out!"

"I said put her down."

"And I said get out of my way!"

Fortunately, several of Jordan's men rushed to help him carry her out of the airport and into Jordan's waiting limousine.

"I'm being kidnapped," Gini screamed, with five video cameras recording every detail.

Jordan pulled Gini inside, and the limousine hurtled through the darkness with the speed of a bullet.

"Where are you taking me?" she asked in a low, pleading voice. She lifted her face from the leather upholstery. Shock waves quaked through her at his tough treatment.

She caught a glimpse of his carved profile. Midnight-black hair, bronzed skin stretched over rough-hewn bone structure, the ruthless set of his mouth, all struck her forcefully.

He stared out the window at the lights rushing by, giving her no answer.

After only a short distance, the car stopped and Jordan's steel hand clamped around her wrist and forced her outside onto the pavement. His Lear jet stood on the runway.

Savagely he yanked her around and she found herself facing him. Perspiration was beaded on his brow; his powerful body was tight with rage.

"If you think I'm going to fly anywhere with you when you're like this—" she began.

His hard voice sliced across her trembling words. "That's exactly what you're going to do."

Part of her couldn't help cowering from the terrible rage in his eyes.

He jerked her even closer against his body. She tried to struggle, but it was no use. The punishing force of his mouth captured hers, muffling her cry of protest. Behind the brutal possession, Gini sensed his agonized desire as well as his anger at himself for still wanting her. He crushed her against himself. Her legs were glued against his muscled thighs, her breasts flattened against the solidness of his chest.

Then as abruptly as he'd kissed her, he ripped his mouth away.

Her lips felt swollen and bruised, and she brought her hand up to ease the tender pain. The blazing fire of his eyes roamed over her features. He watched the hesitant movement of her fingertips as she traced the throbbing fullness of her mouth.

Every sense in her body clamored in sharp awareness of him, in remembrance of the kiss.

He caught her face in his hands, only this time his touch was gentler, as if even in his anger he regretted hurting her.

"You can't win if you fight me," he said raggedly.

Something in her seemed to break. She felt the power of his large hands cupping her face. He towered over her.

He was right. There was no use in fighting him. She bowed her head in defeat and let him lead her onto the jet.

Only when they were taxiing down the runway did he release her.

"Fasten your seat belt," he commanded grimly.

When she hesitated and rubbed her bruised arms, he leaned over and roughly grabbed the metal ends and fastened them himself.

"What comes next, Jordan? Rape?" Her voice shook, belying her attempt at bravado.

"Damn you, Gini. Don't push me." His fingers grabbed her shoulders digging in mercilessly. "I could almost kill you for what you did tonight. When I saw you dancing with James...I wanted to die. I couldn't stand the thought of you with another man. I wished I'd never met you, never believed in you, never found you again." He stared into her terrified eyes, and at last he relaxed his grip. "But I could never hurt you."

"If you hate me, why did you come after me?"

"I never said I hate you. I only hate myself because I can't despise you as you deserve."

With that he turned and left her, joining the pilot in the cockpit.

Gini passed the long, lonely hours in silent misery. A long time later they landed somewhere and refueled. With Jordan lounging watchfully against the only exit, Gini looked out the window at the lights and the men working on the jet and tried in vain to figure out where they were.

Then there were more hours of black nothingness outside the windows of the jet. She had no idea where he was taking her, nor what he planned to do once they got there.

Sometime in the night she fell into a troubled sleep. When she awoke, she was wrapped in a blanket and a pillow was beneath her head. The jet was bouncing along a rough runway.

Drowsily she looked out the window. A dense gray sky hovered low over velvet green fells. Ribbons of mist floated up from the damp ground and blurred the edges of the hills with their gray protruding crags.

Then it came to her. They were in Scotland.

Heavy footsteps resounded on the winding stone stairs outside the castle's library. With a thudding heart, Gini looked up expectantly from the ancient illuminated volume she had been studying. Jordan threw the oak door open and stepped inside, his awesome male presence dominating the room.

He wore jeans and a thick wool turtleneck sweater just as she did. A faint sheen of dampness clung to his black hair and his sweater, and he hadn't bothered to remove his muddy Wellington boots. He obviously had been outside, though she hadn't seen him, and she'd just come in herself from a long walk.

For two days he had avoided her except during meals, which were silent, awkward affairs. She imagined he must be doing some kind of legwork preparing for the video he was going to make, but she was too proud and too stubborn to ask. She knew the crew wasn't coming for a week.

Jordan allowed her complete freedom of the castle and its grounds. There was no danger of escape since the stark, many turreted castle was on a rocky island. Jordan had her passport, and everybody she'd met on her long walks about the lush green island worked for him. They were too glad of work that paid well to quarrel with the man responsible for it.

Aware of his eyes following her, Gini moved restlessly to the narrow window and pushed it open. The air was crisp with heather and pine. Several Highland cattle grazed on a distant meadow. A lean-nosed sheep-dog was barging headlong down a steep slope toward a path that led to the village. Far away the Atlantic crashed against granite cliffs. If only she and Jordan weren't at war with each other, the setting would have been romantic.

The view did not really distract her from the ominous silence in the room. At last she turned and faced him, asking caustically, "To what do I owe the pleasure of this unexpected visit? Do you intend to haul me to some new jail that is even more remote?"

"I might if I thought it would do any good." His voice was tight to conceal his tension.

"Then I'll start packing."

"Don't bother." His glittering black eyes were menacing, the line of his mouth ruthless. He strode toward her, coming to an abrupt halt six inches from her. "Since you're determined to destroy our relationship, I'm through trying to save it. I went crazy, wild...when I saw you dancing with James. Then you left with him, and I had to know why you wanted every gossip columnist in L.A. to print that you'd run off with him. You deliberately wanted to make me look like a fool to the world. It wasn't enough to leave. You wanted to damage my career."

"No!" she cried.

"Then why?"

When she answered him with silence, something inside him exploded. He seized her by the arm and yanked her roughly against him. The breath was knocked from her lungs by the brutal contact with his muscular chest. "Why, damn you?"

"Because I don't want to live with you, Jordan. And I didn't know any other way to make you hate me enough to let me ago."

Slowly his grip on her arms relaxed and she was able to wrench free. She collapsed shaking against the windowsill. But Jordan wasn't quite through with her, and he stalked her, stretching his arms on either side of her, trapping her.

"Well, you can go now," he growled, his proud fury barely held in check. "Anytime you want. If I'm wrong for you, if my life-style is wrong for you, then so be it. My attorney will be contacting you about child support arrangements and custody for Melanie. I won't try to take her away from you, but naturally I'd like to see her at regular intervals."

"Naturally," she murmured faintly, unable to meet the steel black quality of his eyes.

"Gini, I tried to show you I'm not some kind of immoral freak that happens to be famous. Maybe I'm a rock star, but I try to lead a decent life. Hell, I give more than half of my income to charity. But I can't change who I am—even for you."

With that he turned and walked away. When she looked up, he was at the door. "You only have to tell my pilot, and he'll fly you wherever you want to go."

Then he was gone, and Gini was more wretchedly alone than she'd ever been in her life. The stone walls of the library closed in upon her like the cruelest prison. Her heart beat in wild torment. She dabbed at her eyes that were quickly filling with hot tears.

How was she going to live without him? The years ahead seemed to stretch endlessly. She choked back a sob.

She would go on, somehow, because she had to. The tears began to pour down her cheeks.

Numbly she climbed down to the charming bedroom, with its centuries-old antiques. She threw the clothes Jordan had brought for her into a duffel bag, not caring if she wrinkled them. Then she slung the bag over her shoulder and went down to find Jordan's pilot.

She was outside the castle walls when she heard the melancholy guitar notes echoing in the foggy stillness. The music seemed to be coming from the garden. It drew her like a magnet.

Gini set the bag down on the stone steps and wandered down a gravel path toward the hollow that protected the castle's magnificent garden. Ancient spruce and larch trees lined the path.

The haunting resonance of Jordan's deep voice crooning above the thrumming guitar came to her, and she stopped, listening spellbound.

After you've gone, I don't know what I'm gonna do.
You made the difference in a life that made no difference 'til you.

She started to turn and go back to the castle to get her
bag and leave, but the throbbing anguish in his voice held
her.

Jordan stopped singing. There was only the faint
strumming of his guitar. Then that too died, and there was
only the lonesome sound of the wind stirring the trees.

Standing in the damp forest with the dew dripping from
the leaves, Gini remembered the pain in the other song he
had written because of her, "In Every Stranger's Face."

One line came back to her. "Lonely days and lonely
nights have been my fate."

Jordan hadn't been lying when he'd written that. He'd
had Felicia. He'd had money, and he'd had fame. And it
hadn't been enough. It still wasn't. If she left him, she
condemned him to that fate.

Suddenly Gini realized she was acting like a child, just
as she'd done all those years ago. She was running because she was too scared to stay and fight for the man she
loved. She was afraid of his world, afraid of glamorous
women like Felicia. Gini wasn't leaving because she was
afraid of holding him back. He was a star. She was leaving because she was too afraid to stay.

But wasn't she being selfish not to listen to him? He had
been lonely until he'd brought her back to California. She
remembered his pleasure in at last having a family.

If she left, what genuine friend would he have? She
thought of Fawna and Clay. Clay, with his tendency to
marry unwisely, seemed to frustrate Jordan more than
anything else.

Jordan had his band. His music. He had Felicia, who didn't really love him. He had the palace Felicia had built for him.

Gini realized that Jordan really did need her, and it was a thrilling revelation. Imagine being needed by a man as extraordinary as Jordan!

If she left him, she would destroy his chance for personal happiness as surely as she destroyed her own.

Oh, why had she been such a fool? Why hadn't she realized a long time ago that no one gets exactly what he bargains for in life? A person has to be willing to accept his life and work out the problems. Maybe she hadn't asked to fall in love with a man who became a celebrity, but if she turned her back on him now it would be a destructive act of cowardice.

Hesitantly she made her way through the thick trees to the garden.

At first he didn't see her. He was slumped on the bench in the center of the garden, looking down at the now-silent guitar in his lap.

She stared at him lovingly for a long moment. Then she kicked a piece of gravel with the toe of her shoe.

"Jordan..."

He looked up, the pain and joy in his luminous black eyes dazzling her as he silently communicated the terrible force of his love for her. Something in her eyes must have spoken to him, because he arose slowly. Then they were both running.

They were in each other's arms.

Jordan enfolded her in a crushing embrace. Gini felt alive again, wildly alive and happy.

"Jordan, I want to stay... if you'll have me after what I did," she said hesitantly at last.

She heard him take a quick breath.

"If?" He kissed her lips tenderly, eagerly.

She had begun to tremble with fierce, overwhelming emotion. Her arms lifted around his shoulders, her fingertips brushing the soft black hair that curled against his neck.

After a long time, he released her lips.

"I—I only did what I did to make you jealous and angry. I heard you talking to Felicia on the beach. I imagined you kissing her...."

"I didn't," he muttered thickly, caressing her cheek. "I told her I loved you."

"When I heard you talking I decided you two did belong together. She'd done so much for your career. I thought if I publicly humiliated you, you would have to let me go, and that in the long run my going would be the right thing for you and for your career."

"Oh, Gini. When are you going to learn that my career isn't everything, that being a celebrity isn't everything? Yes, Felicia has done a lot for me, and I'll always be grateful to her. I care about her, but I love you. I want you and Melanie, Gini. If I could only have you two, I would be the happiest man in the world."

"And I want you. It's just that I feel so ordinary, so out of place in your world. I thought Felicia was the right woman, and that if I left, you two could find each other again."

"You're the only woman I want, and you're extraordinary, Gini, in your own way. Your love for me is extraordinary. It lasted thirteen years, didn't it? Who else would have gone on loving me as you did?"

"I couldn't stop myself."

"Gini, being a celebrity isn't what's important. Nor is not being one. It's the kind of person you are. You're so beautiful and passionate, so loving and gentle. No one has ever given me the kind of devotion and unquestioning loyalty you're capable of. You enrich my life more than I can ever repay. That, my darling, is extraordinary.''

Gini's eyes met his, and suddenly she felt blissfully happy. It would be up to her to find something to do with her life. Perhaps she would enroll at UCLA and study film-making, but that would be in the future. For now, Jordan's love was enough.

Jordan clasped both her hands in his and, holding them in his sure, hard grip as if he never wanted to let her go, he said gently, ''Maybe it was better that we lost each other the way we did, for thirteen years. Those first years in my career were so chaotic we might have been torn apart by all the pressures. Now, I've gotten to the place where I can make my own terms. I don't have to go on tour. If you don't like Malibu, we can live anywhere we want.''

''Malibu's all right, Jordan. Anywhere. So long as I'm with you.''

He gazed at her so intently she was certain he could see her soul.

''I want you to be my wife again, and this time your answer had better be yes.''

She laughed softly, joyfully. ''That goes without saying.''

And those words were the last words either of them spoke for a very long time.

His hard lips took hers again, and he wanted much more than a kiss.

𝒟 Silhouette Desire
COMING NEXT MONTH

SECOND WIFE—Stephanie James
Was even friendship too much to expect from Heather after what Flynn had done? He'd loved, then left her, but he soon learned that she was too irresistible for him to stay away.

BRANDED—Gina Caimi
Reporter Ross Baxter assumed it would be easy to trap Sharon Farrell into admitting her husband's death had been no accident. But Ross found himself caught in quite a different trap: love.

NOT AT EIGHT, DARLING—Sherryl Woods
If network VP Michael Compton rescheduled Barrie MacDonald's sitcom out of prime time, the results could be disastrous. Would the magnetic attraction they felt for each other last beyond the season?

LOVE MEDICINE—Suzanne Carey
Diana had been drawn to Rafe years before, but her father had come between them. When the two of them reunited, the feelings were still there, and now they could overcome the obstacles in their path.

BITTERSWEET HARVEST—Leslie Davis Guccione
Six Irish brothers against one lone woman hardly seemed fair, but Andrew Branigan was willing to do anything to keep Holly from selling her land to developers—and to convince her of his love.

CALIFORNIA COPPER—Joan Hohl
The second book in Joan Hohl's Trilogy for Desire. Sculptor Zachery Sharp, the identical twin of the hero of Texas Gold (Desire #294) meets singer Aubrey Mason, the woman who makes him whole.

AVAILABLE NOW:

IN EVERY STRANGER'S FACE
Ann Major

STAR LIGHT, STAR BRIGHT
Naomi Horton

DAWN'S GIFT
Robin Elliott

MISTY SPLENDOR
Laurie Paige

NO PLAN FOR LOVE
Ariel Berk

RAWHIDE AND LACE
Diana Palmer

ATTRACTIVE, SPACE SAVING BOOK RACK

Display your most prized novels on this handsome and sturdy book rack. The hand-rubbed walnut finish will blend into your library decor with quiet elegance, providing a practical organizer for your favorite hard-or soft-covered books.

Only $9.95

**Approximately
16" x 8"
when assembled**

Assembles in seconds!

To order, rush your name, address and zip code, along with a check or money order for $10.70 ($9.95 plus 75¢ postage and handling) (New York residents add appropriate sales tax),payable to *Silhouette Reader Service* to:

In the U.S.

Silhouette Reader Service
Book Rack Offer
901 Fuhrmann Blvd.
P.O. Box 1325
Buffalo, NY 14269-1325

Offer not available in Canada.

BKR-2

Silhouette Desire

Available
October 1986

California Copper

The second in an exciting new
Desire Trilogy by Joan Hohl.

If you fell in love with Thackery—the
laconic charmer of *Texas Gold*—you're
sure to feel the same about his twin
brother, Zackery.

In *California Copper*, Zackery meets the
beautiful Aubrey Mason on the windswept
Pacific coast. Tormented by memories,
Aubrey has only to trust...to embrace
Zack's flame...and he can ignite the fire in
her heart.

The trilogy continues when you
meet Kit Aimsley, the twins' half
sister, in *Nevada Silver*. Look for
Nevada Silver—coming soon from
Silhouette Books.